I0566658

Swim Team

Everly Chappelle

Copyright © 2014 Everly Chappelle
All rights reserved.
ISBN-10: 0692287345
ISBN-13: 978-0692287347 (Swim Team)

For Ellen.

AKNOWLEDGMENTS

Cover design by Erin Brock

Cover photo by Christo Brock

Cover modeled by Tim Rusch

Edited by S. Christian

Prologue

The backdoor creaked downstairs and I froze where I stood, feather duster in hand. I looked around and saw the bed I had just made with new zillion-count cotton linens. The afternoon sun shone through the bay window from across the room. I was on the second floor of the Victorian home. There was nowhere to go.

My tiny sundress barely skimmed the top of my thigh. I cautiously fingered the lace atop my breasts.

Had he found the key hidden in the plant on the wrap-around porch? The footsteps I heard were heavy and careless. *A man*, I thought. I envisioned his shoes scratching the original hardwood floors that I had just refinished.

I didn't waver as I listened to him plod around twenty feet below me. Pots and pans rattled against the soapstone countertop. Something metal made a sliding sound against something else that I wasn't able to make out. *Was he sharpening a blade?*

The kitchen would be defiled when I next saw it. The thought of it made my skin crawl.

Drawers and cabinets clamored open and closed in the office. It was quiet and then papers tousled around before falling into a messy heap. For an instant, I pictured the disarray he created downstairs and felt annoyance. He cleared his throat and I could feel the tendons of my own tighten.

Moments later, I heard a creak. He was on the staircase. My pulse began to race. I clutched the duster tight and pushed it forward to nudge the bedroom door closed. The handle clicked into place and bounced back out. There was a small gap between the door and its frame. I didn't look through. Instead, I sucked in a breath and waited.

For a moment, there was no sound. The dirty wand lay sewn into my fingers as I tried not to rock in place.

I heard them; footsteps again – in the hallway – outside the bedroom door. The cat meowed and ran. Her claws scraped on the wood as she slid in a panic to seek refuge in the guest room. There was a bang on the wall.

He shoved through the entrance and stood at attention, surveying the soft warm colors of the bedroom. I gasped at the sight of his black ski mask drowned in sunlight. I stared, my body still. He met my gaze. His eyes danced as my eyes widened.

I couldn't make out the features in his face, but I noticed the excitement in his oversized pupils and the arousal in his slacks. The intruder's deltoids pushed at the tight material of the grey undershirt he wore. He was built with broad shoulders; a body that could easily snap mine in half.

"Take anything you want," I told him, "Please don't hurt me." I whimpered and covered my chest with my free hand. My nipples were hard.

He grunted and zeroed in on the flesh framed by the lace atop the almost sheer sundress. The man took a heavy breath. He reached out and pulled my palm and outspread fingers from my chest. His lips parted and he made a low guttural sound before moving to my other hand. Wrapping his fingers around the wand, he slid the duster from between my fingertips. I was hypnotized, releasing my death grip as if under a spell brought on by his musky scent.

His pupils were engorged, covering almost all of his eyes. I wished he would have removed his ski mask so I could see a human face rather than stare into the dark abyss of the black-eyed predator.

His free hand found mine and pulled me to him. I conceded like a lamb. He leaned toward my neck and inhaled my rose scented perfume. My feet attempted to step backward, but he wouldn't allow it. He grabbed my wrist and turned my arm in itself, forcing my body to revolve in the direction he now wanted me – his prey; his meal.

His left hand burned the flesh of my wrist, while his fingertips on the right hand slid down my free arm. I pushed at his chest in vain.

I protested softly, "Please, don't." As I attempted to step back again, the metal edge of the bed frame forced my knees to buckle and my butt cheeks found a seat on the fluffy 0bedding that I had washed and made only hours before.

He stood between my thighs – a wolf. "Quiet," he said in a low, sultry voice.

My chin tilted back and I stretched my free hand up to pull his mask off his face. The wolf was quick. He stopped my hands mid-stretch and flung them back down.

"You are so-"

I felt the sting of his slap before I saw his hand flying toward my face. My body instantly heated and responded. Pricks of pain flushed my cheek. My nerves were on alert.

"I said, 'quiet!'" He covered my mouth with his large palm. His eyes were momentarily crazed. "Do what I say and no one gets hurt, Lady."

"Yes, Mister." I gave in to his command, "Please don't hurt me. I'll do anything you want."

At this he grinned. I could see his biceps dancing in his arms.

"Turn over," he said gruffly. I began to move, but he flipped me to a prone position before I could get to my elbows. He took a fistful of my hair a pulled at my head forcing my back to arch. I felt his heated breath through my thin clothing.

The wolf ran his large hands down my sides, feeling the curves of my body. He stopped at my ass and gave it a double-fisted grab, followed by a smack that stung worse than the slap a moment ago.

He took off his shirt and refocused on me. The wolf pulled the skirt of my dress up to my waist and traced his index down my inner thigh. I felt his hot breath on my backside as he slowly kissed down my right leg and back up the left one. His coarse chest hair brushed along the back of my knee. He paused, pulling my thighs apart to make room for his face.

Kissing me through my thong made me hot and wet. I was dying to feel his tongue on my swollen pink skin. His lips lingered a moment longer, driving me crazy before he finally moved the damp lace of my undergarment aside and slide his tongue along my labia.

He licked, kissed and fingered me from my rear until I was screaming and panting. Just before I came, he released himself from my flesh.

"Hey!" I panted, confused.

In one fell swoop, my dress was over my head and I was on my back. The predator was on top of me, still in his pants. "You want it?" he asked.

"Yes, baby." *I was his lamb. He could do anything he wanted.*

He backed away and stood up, undoing his belt.

"Give it to me," I said.

The wolf unleashed his belt and doubled it up in his hand. That was going to leave a mark, I thought, sarcastically. I knew what was coming.

He let one end of the leather whip loose and ripped into my side. (I rolled right as he got me.)

"Why'd you move?" He growled.

"Because that shit hurts."

"Hmmm," was all he said.

"Why don't you grab my hair and I'll pretend to be scared," I encouraged him.

The wolf grunted again and rolled his eyes.

I took his hand and placed it on a few strands of hair. A moment passed before he took the bait. He grabbed a mess of hair and pulled me to a seated position.

He stood up. "You gonna give me a show?" I teased.

"Shut up, Bitch," he instructed without looking up. The wolf unzipped his pants and dropped his trousers, exposing himself to me. His manhood stood at attention. He instructed me to suck it. I nodded and knelt down, using my hand to slide his dick into my mouth.

He sighed and pushed himself further into the warmth of my mouth.

I could feel tension release his body. With little trouble, I moved him from his feet to his back. I moved on top of him, swirling my tongue around his hard shaft. My face bobbed forward and back, taking him in deep and then easing out again, repeatedly. My husband moaned beneath me and removed his ski cap.

He released himself from my lips and pulled my flushed face up to his. (Our little attack scenario was forgotten.) "That was fucking awesome," he said as he panted beneath me. The ends of my hair tickled the sides of his face. I watched him smile as he brushed the strands aside and pulled my lips to his.

We each took a breath, looked deep into one another's eyes and made love the way most people imagine doing it, only, I'd like to believe, it was sweeter.

It was perfect. Everything was so perfect back then.

1

It was the first day of a new semester. I slid into a staff parking spot with ease and as my right heel pressed into the asphalt, I could feel my foot start to sweat.

I had been teaching at the University in the desert for the past year and still felt like an outsider from the east. People kept telling me that I'd get used to the dry heat, but I hadn't taken to it yet.

My skin melted below my blazer. Yes, *the blazer*. It was my good luck charm; part of my teaching uniform. Plus, it was one hundred ten degrees in the sun and ten below freezing in the classroom. I needed layers.

I grabbed my laptop bag and almost closed the car door when I realized that my coffee was still in the center console. I reached in and yanked it out haphazardly with my free arm. When I pulled back the lid popped off the cup and lukewarm coffee spewed into the air like decorative droplets tossed from a fountain, only the color of mud. Before I could react, the coffee plummeted onto my jacket, creating an array of brown circular markings.

That was the start of a less-than-wonderful day. I put on a good front and faked my way through two classes. The undergraduates in my classes must have thought that I was either trampy or crazy, teaching in the fitted white t-shirt, trendy dark jeans and strappy heels.

After class, I stopped to stare in the bathroom mirror. *Son of a bitch!* I swore to myself. My round breasts, covered by a navy blue bra, had been exposed through the thin white cotton. Yes, they were lovely breasts, but the students need not get the whole show the first day of class.

They think I'm a whore, I worried. What I needed was to relax and let go of the hostile feelings I was having over the coffee that assaulted my attire. So, in lieu of walking east toward my office, I headed in the opposite direction.

The lap pool at school, offered the ultimate escape from the real, coffee-stained world. The advantage of working at this relatively new University is that the Runnin' Rebel Athletic complex is up-to-date, clean and spacious. The athletes have the best of all the latest and greatest sports equipment.

I showed my ID to the attractive young athlete manning the front desk to the PE building. He smiled and winked. I was surprised by his attention, but then I remembered that I was wearing that damned tight shirt. I decided to take it as a compliment, smiled at the boy and went about my business.

The locker room was empty so I checked myself out in the full-length mirror. I wore a red, two-piece Speedo. It's a swimsuit that says, "I'm athletic and strong, yet curvy and feminine." It supports the chest and allows its wearer to show off her hard earned abdominal muscles.

Yup, not too shabby, I thought as I flexed my stomach in the mirror. The door to the locker room creaked a warning that other people were entering the premises. I turned from my reflection and grabbed my towel.

At the pool's edge, I put on my super cool goggles and slipped into the moderately warm water of the nearest open lane. Arm over arm, I thrust forward. My legs, part of the machine, beat at the water. Within a few strokes, I found my groove.

Moving through the pool instantaneously takes me back in time to a happier era of my life. It's a huge part of why I'm addicted to swimming. The physical high is the other part.

My lungs drew in efficient breaths of air as I worked out my body. It was sheer bliss. The outside world melted away, just as sound dissipates under water. My mind purged itself of present thought and shifted to fond memories and feelings of the past. There was once a time when I thought, *This is it! It doesn't get any better!*

It had been a quite a while since I'd felt that type of satisfaction and general lust for life; not since I was in Pennsylvania.

After thirty minutes, I paused on the side of the pool for a break. I pulled off my goggles and cleaned them in the water before setting them on the deck. I stretched my shoulders, using the side of the pool as a lever. My body felt good. I took another breath, glanced around the room and spotted a familiar face.

It was Craig. He was walking toward my side of the pool. His body was dry, but chiseled as only a swimmer's body could be. He was lean and broad. But, he was a younger version of his self.

But it wasn't Craig. *Man, I really thought it was him for a moment,* I reflected as I refocused my eyes.

He stepped to the edge of the lane next to me and began to stretch his chest and shoulders. He bent forward and did a few knee bends. His face was only feet from mine.

Wait a minute! I know this kid!

"Hey!" I said in a happy tone, "I know you."

He smiled a crooked grin and flashed a set of big white teeth. I could tell he still didn't recognize me.

"You're in my speech class," I clarified, "I mean, I'm your teacher, Mrs. Templeton."

"Oh yeah." he stepped to the edge and put out his hand, which I shook.

"I'm sorry, but I didn't catch your name today," I admitted.

"I'm Todd," he said.

"Nice to meet you, Todd."

"Back at ya."

He paused before opening his mouth again, "So you're a swimmer, Professor Templeton?" Todd asked me as if it were an alien type thing for a teacher to be so ballsy as to leave the walls of the building in which she taught. I could also swear I heard a hint of admiration underneath his words. Swimming was the thing I was best at. I was glad that he had noticed my stroke.

"Yes, Todd. I do swim. I do a lot of things. In fact, when I was your age I was on my college's swim team." I told him, entertained by his interest.

"That's pretty tight, Professor! It's really good that you're doing so much to stay in shape at your age."

At your age? I echoed in my mind. *Ouch!*

"Yeah, If more older people kept in shape the way you do–"

"Yeah, Todd. I got it!" I cut him off, embarrassed and offended. Just how old did he think I was?

"I'm on the UNLV swim team," he proceeded to tell me.

"Excellent," I commended him and hoped he didn't hear the undertone of annoyance in my voice. "Have a good swim," I said, turning to face my lane. My arms shot over my head as I glided over the black line on the floor of the pool. I started swimming freestyle and forced myself to forget about the boy swimming in the lane next to me who all but called me, "old."

I am not old! I could pass for twenty-five easily! *I swear!* Just last week a lady at Vons carded me for a bottle of wine.

After ten more laps, I was pooped and popped up onto the pool deck. Todd was breaking to chat with the guy in the lane on the other side. I waved to him as I got to my feet.

"Have a good day, Professor Templeton," he said with that lop-sided smile.

"Thanks, Todd. And, by the way, it's *Mrs.* Templeton. I'm not a Professor," I leaned forward to correct him.

I saw him check out my chest, so I stood back up. Then he clearly eyed the tummy, which I had worked so hard for.

He popped out of the water and stepped toward me. "Doesn't the team work-out in the morning?" I asked as an attempt to stop the almost naked young man from moving any closer.

It worked. He paused as if in thought for a moment. Then he looked at me quizzically before stating, "Coach wasn't at practice today, so we all went home to catch up on some sleep."

"Coach Sutton?" He had been a coach at Penn State while I was there. "He didn't call or show up? That doesn't sound like him at all."

Todd gazed off to the right, "I know...weird."

"Have you spoken with him?"

"No."

"Has anyone?"

"I don't know. But, we had a team dinner last night. Maybe he drank too much. Anyway, I'm sure he'll tell us what happened at tomorrow's practice," Todd didn't appear very concerned. But, I was. My husband and Coach had been close for years. He was also at Coach's house last night.

"You're probably right," I agreed with him, but made a mental note to call Coach later.

"Well... I better get back in the water, Miss Templeton," He flashed the grin.

"Mrs. Templeton," I corrected.

"You don't look like a *Mrs.*," he overtly eyed me up and down.

"Well I am and I'm your teacher," I stood tall and stepped toward the insolent boy.

"I can change classes," he smiled.

"I'm the only speech teacher at this school. Sooner or later you'll have to take my course," I told him in my teacher voice.

"That sucks." He locked in on my eyes and stepped another step closer. Todd smiled. My nerves stood at attention.

"Catch ya later, *Teach*," he said. He turned abruptly away and popped back into the lap pool. Before I could pick my jaw back up, he was doing the butterfly.

Still got it! I thought as a glow of delight washed through me. I stood looking at the swimmer in a bit of a trance. He turned at the wall and started swimming back my way. I snapped out of the stupor and turned my back to him, walking out before he could hit the wall again.

2

I parked in front of our two-level stucco house and felt a wave of longing for the historic brick home we used to own. Built at the turn of the century, it had personality and wasn't the same color as every other house on the block. Countless times, I have tried to open the wrong garage before realizing that I was trying to get into someone else's cream-colored home, complete with obligatory cactus planter and plastic grass in the front yard.

Some other couple was enjoying our New England home now. I pictured its façade as I turned they key to the front door. I dropped my tote bag in the foyer, all but forgetting about the laptop inside.

My cat, Puddles, gave me a skeptical look. (Yes, she pees where she shouldn't pee.) Her ears twitched as she cocked her head. She took careful steps as she walked into the hallway before stopping to meow.

"Its okay," I reassured her, "He's not with me."

"Meow," said Puddles. I squatted down to pet her before going to change into some soft, pink sweats.

Puddles and I sank into the couch, happy to be home alone to enjoy the four episodes of *America's Next Top Model* that I had Tivo'd. There was a laundry list of productive things I should have been doing, but instead, I opted to indulge in something of absolutely no value other than sheer entertainment. It gave me a little thrill. Watching TV was the most naughty thing I'd done in a long time.

We'd just finished the second episode when Puddles jumped off my lap. Craig's keys jingled in the lock on the outer side of the front door. I pressed the "off" button on TV remote and tossed it on the couch to hide the evidence of my indulgence.

"Hi Baby!" said the voice of the man that I had been in love with since my sophomore year of college.

"Hi Pumpkin!" I smiled and turned to see his tall figure in the entryway. He smiled and, in turn, I smiled back even bigger. His smile was infectious and impossible to resist. Unconsciously, I ran my fingers through my hair as I watched my husband in the large, open foyer.

Craig set his briefcase down next to my bag and walked over to kiss my head. It brought me back to my childhood. My Dad would kiss the top of my head when he came home from his job at the bank. Lately, my husband's kisses had been feeling more and more incestuous, rather than like kisses exchanged by lovers.

We had been so passionate when we were in college! Craig and I were both on the swim teams at Pennsylvania State. I saw him at the pool working out, the first week of my freshman year and I lusted after him for the entire semester. Though a bit geeky, I thought he was the hottest guy on the team.

I watched him from afar, planning my own swim schedule so that I would be walking into the pool complex as he was leaving just so I could smile and catch his eye to say, "Hi."

I noticed him at the cafeteria. He seemed so *nice*. He spoke to all the workers and seemed to know every person who walked into the crowded room. Everyone liked him. I thought a guy like *that*; a guy who *everyone* knew and *everyone* liked was out of my league. He was Mr. Personality and I was just me.

I wasn't shy, although I wasn't the type to initiate friendships. What I had going for me were my looks, intelligence and sense of humor. (Craig might disagree about the "sense of humor" part. My sarcasm escapes him.) I just didn't feel like I was special enough for him. In short, I was a girl of eighteen, lacking the confidence that I had eventually matured into.

He was a year my senior and I didn't know it, but he secretly had a crush on me too. He didn't think of me the way I thought of myself. He saw that I was special. And, as he told me later, he was too nervous to go up and talk to me. Mr. Personality could talk to anyone and everyone on campus, but not to me.

Fate and school schedules brought us together. We ended up in the biology class with a few other swim team members. Anyone who has ever taken Biology 101, knows that the only way to pass is to form a study group. So, through the miracle of schoolwork, we came together.

I showed up at his apartment to study along with six other swimmers. He was so sweet to me. He kept offering me drinks and sat next to me in our study circle. I thought it was a coincidence until he brushed the side of his arm against mine. It was warm and soft. I felt my face blush and forced myself to resist the urge to look at him.

I pressed my pencil into my notebook and tried to write down what the "smart" guy in our group was saying. Then, I felt the side of his leg press to my thigh. It sent a shock through my body, igniting my senses.

There was no use trying to listen. All my body's senses were overloaded by his closeness. My ears rang. I nonchalantly turned my head toward the older boy next to me.

"I'm sorry," he said and moved his leg apart from mine.

Instantly, I regretted turning to face him. He had taken it to mean I was bothered. I would have preferred to sit all night with his leg pressed to mine, not looking at him, than to have had it severed from its new mate.

I smiled. "No problem," I said, trying to appear casual. But, it was gone. I missed his touch and longed to feel it again. My focus returned to the notebook on my lap.

Then, the warmth came back. This time it was his hand on my knee. "Would you pass me the pretzels," he asked as if it were the most natural thing in the world to touch someone and send sensational pulses through their legs. I felt the hair on my arms rise.

I handed him the pretzels and made eye contact in the process. He gave me the most amazing look any boy had ever given me. My insides melted to mush. I returned the look and felt my mouth smile. I wished I could play it cool, but he had me. I was his. He could have done anything to me that night and I would have let him. But, he didn't.

When the others left, he found a reason for me to lag behind. He took me back to his room to show whatever it was. It didn't matter once we were alone. Our legs found each other and intertwined. Our lips met and parted to allow our saliva to meet.

Our fingers explored each others' flesh. I never wanted it to end. The thought of parting my body from his killed me. One big thing stood in our way, though.

I had to tell him. He would certainly know soon had I let things continue on the path we were on. I separated my mouth from his and took a breath. He stared into my eyes. It was hypnotic and I found myself kissing him again. We wrapped ourselves even tighter and found the bed.

He began to remove my top and my nerves took over. I pulled back and looked away from his trance-inducing gaze. "I've never done this before," I said almost under my breath.

"What?" he whispered.

"I mean, I want to do it, but I think you should know that I'm a virgin," I peered up to his eyes to gauge his response.

He reached his fingers to my forehead and brushed my hair back behind my ear. "You are so beautiful, Susan" he told me.

I stared at him not knowing what to say back to the boy I had admired all semester.

"We can wait until you are ready," he announced and wrapped his arms around me pulling me close.

I kissed his chest. I feared that the night would end and I would never get a chance to be so close to my fantasy boy. "I'm ready now," I declared and began to suck on his lower lip.

He smiled, popping out of my lip lock. "I can't believe I'm saying this, but let's just cuddle, okay?"

"But, I want to have sex with you," I said becoming more confident about my need to be with him.

"Tomorrow, okay?"

"Really?" I rested my cheek to his chest.

"Sure, or the next. We don't need to rush the rest of our lives." He played with my hair until I fell asleep. We cuddled and made out every night that week. Craig was right. It was the perfect start to the rest of our lives.

And the rest was easy. Craig and I finished college. We moved in together and got married. Then, we stayed at the same college and worked on our next degrees. Later, we both got jobs teaching at the very same college. Craig taught biology, ironically, and I taught speech.

We had a great sex life and exciting mini-adventures on the weekends. Our friends were awesome. We adored them and they loved us. A group of us from college stayed tight and took turns hosting soirées at our homes for each other. Life was so perfect...so good!

Craig got his PhD. immediately after finishing his Masters. He really is "Professor Templeton." I took a break from school after my graduate degree and began to pay off my loans by teaching.

Life was so good before. We had security, familiarity, family and momentum. Then he convinced me to move.

He came home so excited the day he got the offer. It was impossible not to get caught up in his joy. He was so happy. It was overwhelming. So when he told me that he got a job offer at a new University for a better salary and a shot at a more exciting life, I squealed.

Professor Templeton was glowing with exultation! He got me all keyed up about the possibility of a fun new adventure. I wanted him to feel that way forever. There was no way I was going to take it from him. So, we moved to Sin City.

What I didn't think about or plan on was the remorse I would feel over the life I had to give up in order to give my husband the life he wanted.

I felt guilty about my feelings of blame. And I was disappointed in myself for disliking our life in Las Vegas. The fact that we had slept together a total of four times in the past six months didn't help either.

Why can't I just be happy for him? I asked myself repeatedly.

Was I jealous?

No. I answered myself. I just wanted to feel how I used to feel – happy.

Craig was *excruciatingly* happy and I was empty inside.

In Pennsylvania, the leaves would be turning soon. There were no leaves in Vegas. He didn't mention our anniversary last week, nor, did he notice my depressed state of being. That was par for the course.

As we'd gotten older, things had changed. Craig was the star of his own show. "It's the *Craig Show*, starring Craig."

I remained on the couch, watching the *Craig Show* in action. I wondered whether or not he might take notice of the fact that I was unhappy. Perhaps he would magically become psychic.

Craig whistled a tune as he sauntered to the kitchen. Oh yes, the guy was happy as a lark.

The cat eyed him from under the table, ready to dart away in an instant.

Craig made me a turkey sandwich with extra Miracle Whip, just like I like it. The cat crouched down as my husband placed the sandwich in my hand. I looked at the food he'd created for me. It had romaine lettuce too? *Fantastic!*

What a wonderful sandwich-making hubby I have, I thought. *I love Craig when he does sweet little things. Maybe he did notice how pathetic I felt today.* Maybe Craig was reaching out to me? Maybe the sandwich was a peace offering. Maybe it was a new beginning.

We sat in front of the TV, the sound turned low, and ate our sandwiches.

"How was your first day of school?" he asked between bites.

"It sucked and it was all your fault," I replied with my mouth full mayonnaise and lettuce.

To this he laughed and wiped a smear of Miracle Whip from my cheek. I ate my sandwich like a piggie. It wasn't as sexy as a Carl's Jr. commercial, but it tasted best that way.

"Seriously, it sucked." I pushed him gently with my free hand. "I got coffee all over my top layer and had to teach the class looking like a tramp in a tight t-shirt."

"I'm sure you looked fine." Craig remarked looking in the direction of the TV. He picked up the remote, changed the channel to ESPN2 and turned up the volume.

"You know I need my costume, my *blazer*, to feel like a teacher." I tried to explain why I was distraught. It was too late. He didn't hear me. I was being overdramatic and he was calm and collected.

That was the end of that heartfelt conversation. I shoved the last bite of the sandwich into my mouth and went upstairs. Puddles trailed at my heels.

Blissfully unaware that my life was in need of a drastic change, Craig reclined his section of the couch backward and enjoyed the *Craig Show*. He probably thought we were doing well, in our relationship, I mean. Sure, we lived together in peace. But, peace meant no fireworks, no flames – no nasty role-play, no toe-curling squeals!

We cohabitated, like roommates, and it bothered me.

Truth be told, I didn't want to know the "why" or the "how." I just needed things to get back to the way they used to be.

3

Craig rolled over and flopped his big, heavy leg on top of my petite little knee. It bore down on my kneecap with gorilla-like pressure. I woke up and threw the giant appendage back to his side of the bed.

Tempting, as it was, to sleep apart from the man whom I had married less than ten years ago, I was not certain that separation was what I wanted. On the one hand, there was the Craig, who carried on blissfully happy, while I quietly lurked about in my dark cloud of discontent. He either didn't notice my depression or he didn't care.

On the other hand, there was the Craig who makes sandwiches; the charismatic Craig whose glowing smile infected all who felt it. He was an attractive, intelligent man. I was proud to walk on his arm. Envy flashed through the eyes of other women when they saw me with him. We did look good together, especially from the outside.

Needless to say, I stayed in our bed, rolled over and turned on the TV. I clicked around and stopped when I saw video of the front of the Athletic Complex, where I swam earlier today. It was the News. They showed a photo of the University's Swim Coach and it had two dates below it, 1953 was the year he was born and the second year was the year that he died, *this year*.

I didn't believe it at first. There was no way the story was real. Coach Sutton wasn't the youngest guy in the world, but he certainly wasn't old enough to pass on. *No, no no! This is a mistake,* I thought, waiting for the newscaster to get a correction and tell the audience that he had been wrong. Coach was just sick. He wasn't dead.

Come on, News Guy, Say it.

He isn't dead!

But the News Person didn't change his story. He just kept on talking and showing sound bites of surprised faculty and kids on campus.

I forced myself to accept that his death was real and watched the rest of the story.

Evidently, Coach Sutton had gotten food poisoning. It happened without warning. He had a large dinner at his home with The Runnin' Rebels Swim Team the night before and woke up with flu-like symptoms. He had slept in, which explained the missed swimming practice.

No one took it very seriously, including him. Coach began puking mid-morning. By the afternoon, there was so much vomit and blood that his wife called an ambulance. By the late afternoon Coach Sutton had passed away. He left behind his lovely younger wife, two grown children and one grade school-aged child.

According to the news reporters, there was no food evidence leftover. It had been thrown out and the roadside trash service took it before the crime scene investigators could get to it for testing. Coach Sutton's widow was bawling. I could see from the video that she really loved him. I mean, *really, passionately* loved him. It was the kind of love so many of us long for; the kind where you cannot possibly go on living without your lover by your side.

Poor Elizabeth Sutton, I thought, wondering whether she blamed herself for her husband's surprising death. After all, she had cooked most of the meal. You can never really know what someone is feeling in that kind of situation, though. Tragedy affects every person so differently. Maybe, I would be angry if I were in her situation. After all, the swim team members had each brought over dishes of food to share that night. And, Coach Sutton was the only one to become ill and die.

Maybe blame was the furthest thing from her mind. Maybe she's just sad.

The whole thing was tragic. Sutton was well-liked. He was a mentor to more than one generation of young swimmers.

I conjured up my favorite memory of Coach Sutton. It was before a swim meet in college. He told the dumbest joke to lighten the mood. Everyone rolled their eyes but him. I could picture his face red from laughing so hard. His small belly bounced up and down until he was out of breath. Sutton was never heavy, but he was a jolly old guy.

Although I had seen him less often since he, and eventually we, had moved to Vegas, I would miss him.

I wasn't looking forward to telling Craig, however. He saw the Suttons much more often than I did. He was at the Sutton house yesterday.

I put my head on the pillow and forced my eyes shut. My mind reeled for a bit, pondering the news story. I visualized the picture from the TV and then images of him from the past. I smiled.

Then I frowned, opening my eyes. It hit me! Coach Sutton had passed away. He was dead and he wasn't coming back.

Not that I could control the salty tears that fell to my lips before I even realized it was happening, but I sat up in bed and allowed myself to cry over Sutton. I mourned his life and I ached for his family's loss.

THE PHONE RANG VERY EARLY. "It's for you," I informed Craig, not daring to open my eyes.

"How do you know? It's still ringing," he wanted to know.

"Coach Sutton died. It's for you." I snuck a look at Craig, searching for his reaction. If my statement shocked him, he sure did a good job at covering it up. His expressionless facade did not surprise me.

My husband, whom had slept soundly while I tossed and turned last night, rolled over and picked up the phone off the night stand. He yawned before greeting the person on the other side.

Often I wonder if Craig is capable of tears, or if he is human at all. He is consistently in control. I've never seen him slip up, as I tend to do. In a situation where I might, shed a tear, his face stays tight. When I would pull at my hair in angst, he would take a light breath and continue on. Where I might gasp, he would only blink. He is a bit of a droid, if you ask me.

This morning, as he hung up the phone, his face was tight. "Coach Sutton died." He told me what I already knew.

"How did you know that before I answered?" Craig wanted to know. He still wasn't crying and that bothered me.

"It was on the news last night. I couldn't sleep."

"Oh," he replied. "It's so weird," was all he could say. Craig wandered into the bathroom and turned on the shower.

He stayed in there a long time. I ended up using the guest shower, which hosted the guest soap and guest shampoo and conditioner. Needless to say, my frizzy hair would not calm down. *I gotta treat my guests better,* I thought after experiencing the fallout using of generic bath products. Then, I remembered that I had no guests. *Boo hoo for me!* Then, I remembered that Coach Sutton was dead and I felt pretty darn stupid for giving a crap what my hair looked like. At least *I* was alive. At least *my husband* hadn't been poisoned to death.

"It's so weird," Craig repeated when he finally emerged from the steamy bathroom. He had locked the door. I wanted to believe that he had been secretly sobbing beneath the sound of the running water. Maybe he does have feelings after all?

"What's wrong with your hair?" He looked at me funny. *He didn't notice when I tried highlights last year, but the sky-high frizz-ball on my head he notices?* I couldn't believe it.

"Don't ask," I said, not wanting to get into it. I walked to the mirror and drowned my locks in anti-frizz goop.

"We were just at his house last month," Craig was doing the math in his head.

"I know. You stopped by his party last night, too."

"I was only there for a second. But, I spoke with him at the pool for a while last week."

"You did?"

"Yeah."

"About what?"

"Oh, you know. Swim stuff. How it used to be. How it is now. How different kids are today, verses when you and I were on the team."

"Well, we went to a very different school than UNLV," I told him.

"That we did."

"Sutton was a good coach."

"Yes, he was."

We stopped talking and each of us went into our own private internal conversations within our imaginations. The house stood quiet as we finished getting ready for work.

I knew that Craig was closer to Sutton than I was. But, we both felt bonded to him. He was Craig's swim coach back at Penn. He was a sort of a mentor to the women's team as well. I looked up to him, just as Craig had.

My chest felt empty, thinking about how easy it was for a life to just disappear. One minute Sutton was breathing, the next he was gone. My nose stung and a bubble rose up in my throat. I felt sad and disoriented, unsure of what to do next. I let a few tears fall and went to work.

*****

I stared at the stack of mini DV tapes on my desk. The day had gone by in a haze. My students had to present speeches for a grade. Usually I grade the speakers as they present in class. Then, I have them take the tape of their speech home and do a self-evaluation for homework.

Today I kept the tapes. I can't remember what excuse I gave the students for keeping the speeches, but they didn't appear to be suspicious.

I knew I should call to offer my condolences to Coach Sutton's widow, but I just couldn't get up the nerve to do it. What if I called and she picked up? What would I say? What if she didn't pick up? What would I say to her voice mail? What if calling was just rude and it were more proper to stop by with a dish of food?

Perhaps sending flowers was a better choice. I could not make up my mind, though, which was odd because I'm not a wishy-washy person. So, instead of dealing with the current situation, I stared at the tapes.

There was a light rap on the open door to my office. I looked up, relieved for the distraction. Todd stood in the doorway. For a brief moment, I saw him as I had at the pool yesterday; shirtless, his chiseled chest muscles uncovered. I must have had a funny look on my face because he didn't walk into the room.

I consciously relaxed the muscles in my face and gestured him in. "Come on in, Todd." I stayed seated waiting for him to get comfortable.

The edges of his mouth quivered as he smiled his crooked smile and walked to the chair in front of my desk. The boy that I knew from the pool, as well as my classroom, looked nervous.

"How's the swim team?" I asked in a far too casual tone before realizing the enormity of my mistake. How dumb could I be? Seriously! *How's the swim team? I am a freakin' idiot! The coach is dead. That' how the swim team is!* I was horrified with my lack of tact! If I could have taken those words back...

He looked down at the floor and squeezed his large eyes closed for a moment.

"I'm sorry. I mean how are you? No, ummm... How can I help you today?" Open mouth, insert foot. My throat seized up and twinged in panic! Speeches, I could do, but this interpersonal communication crap was for the dogs.

I looked down at the floor now, too. I was upset, just like Todd. But, as his teacher, I owed it to him to get it together.

I lifted my face, ran my hand through my hair and sighed, forcing my throat relax. There were no right words to say to him. I said what was on my mind, "I'm an idiot. I'm sorry."

He nodded in acknowledgement and agreement before stating what was weighing on his own mind, "I didn't do very well on my speech today, Professor Templeton."

He looked me in the eyes now and I could see his torment. His watery blue eyes widened. I saw purity, love and pain swimming in the tears he refused to let fall. Todd was so young, sweet and innocent; not yet broken by any of the unbiased cruelties of life. I ached to place my hand on his cheek and tell him that he would be okay, but I was unsure of how he would react to such a gesture.

Instead, I said, "I don't think I did very well on my teaching today, Todd. How about each of us gets a pass on this one?"

"Really? A pass?" He repeated my words in disbelief; "I can redo the speech next week if you want. I can do it better."

"Not necessary."

"Thanks." He did the lop-sided smile again. This was a good-looking guy – boyishly handsome. Generally speaking, I tried not to look at the boy-candy on campus too closely. But, today, I envied whichever eighteen year-old girl got to be with him.

We both stood up. I could feel his utter desolation from across the desk. He was lost and had no one to talk to.

"You know that I knew your Coach?" I offered up a conversation opening.

"You did? How? Through swimming?"

"He coached the men's team at Penn State, where I went to school. He helped my team, the women's team, out from time to time, too."

"It's not fair. He was a good guy. I just spoke with him a day ago. I was at his house." Todd looked down as he continued, "And now he's gone. He was a good man...a good man." Todd let a tear fall down his cheek as he stared down at his hands.

"It's my fault," he mumbled.

I walked around the desk and placed a hand on his large swimmer's shoulder, running my fingers up and down to soothe him. I felt helpless and wished I could make it all better.

"Todd. It is not your fault. There was nothing you could do. No one knew."

He sighed and whimpered; his innocent heart torn. I gave his large deltoid a squeeze.

"No one could have foreseen or prevented this," I told him.

"Thanks," he began to breathe normally again, "I don't know what to do with myself. Swim practice was cancelled again today. None of the guys want to talk about it. They all seem either suspicious, angry or upset."

"Have you been to the Coach's house?" I asked, taking my hand off his shoulder. If it lingered on his body any longer, I might have started touching other parts of him.

"No. Not yet. I'm still working up the courage to go over there. Plus, What am I supposed to bring? Nothing I take to his wife is gonna bring Coach back. Its all so…"

"Awkward." I finished his sentence.

"Yes," he sounded relieved to hear that I felt that way too. He leaned on the edge of my desk and I leaned on the edge next to him. I wondered if he noticed that the sides of our hands touched slightly as we gripped the desk for balance.

We stared forward in silence. I watched an eager student hurry past my open office doorway.

"Well, kiddo, I'll tell you what. I'll go over to the Sutton house if you do." I felt as if we were in the same boat.

"Kiddo? I'm old enough to vote!"

"Great," I said sarcastically, "Are you old enough to drink?"

"Close enough," he said. *Yikes*, I thought, tantalized by the almost of-drinking-age boy next to me.

"So, are you gonna go over to Coach's house?" I asked him.

"No way."

"Really?"

"Not any time soon. I can't face… Maybe after the funeral."

"Oh, geez. I hate funerals. I think I'll wait until after the funeral too. There will be more people around then to buffer any more of my mouth mishaps."

"Yeah, for a speech teacher, you really can get yourself tongue-tied." He smiled at my imperfection.

"Shut-up." I pretended to slap his hand, but barely brushed it.

"You're allright, Templeton." Todd pushed himself off the desk.

"What happened to Professor?"

"I thought you said you weren't a Professor."

"I'm not, but it sounded nice when you said it a moment ago."

"That was when I needed you to give me a good grade on that horrible speech I made. But, I got what I needed." His face lit up and he chuckled a bit.

Todd sauntered to the doorway and I hit him in the chest with the stress ball from my desk. "That will be all then, Burns comma Todd. Office hours are over."

He gave a slanted grin and left.

He was a bit of an impertinent little bugger, but I was glad he left smiling.

4

"They asked me to replace Sutton," my husband announced. We had been sitting in silence, driving to the Sutton home for more than ten minutes.

The funeral, earlier, was full of old nostalgic coaching buddies of Sutton's and many students of his from the past, as well as the present. The service overflowed with men who weren't afraid of tears.

Ironically, I felt uncomfortable in the presence of so many unabashed, choked up males. I fidgeted throughout the service; yet another non-Susanlike flaw rearing its ugly head in the wake of the Sutton tragedy. Why couldn't I keep it together these days? I used to be a much better actress than this unstill, mumbling person who seemed to have taken over control of my body.

I wondered how the kid who thought he was a man was doing. Todd had been pretty disturbed by the whole thing earlier that week, but young people tend to bounce back fairly quickly. Between fidgeting, I looked around for him, but I didn't see Todd's face at the service.

There were hundreds of people at Sutton's funeral. If the Coach could look down from above, I think he'd be happy with the memories he left behind and the lives he had touched. So many people spoke highly of him at the service.

You would think that in a crowd so big, I would recognize quite a few of the people whom I passed by. Apparently, this crowd had the converse effect on my facial recognition software. I walked through the murky sea of unknown faces, unable to pick out those that were familiar.

Sutton's second wife was easy enough to spot, though; young and somber, she sat in the front row, with her smallest child close to her. The grown-up Sutton kids, from marriage number one, huddled next to one another for support on her other side. I couldn't figure out which of the many older women in the audience was his first wife.

We were two blocks from the widow's home when Craig decided to talk. *Great timing!* I indulged him because I needed to know what his answer was. I felt apprehensive for no good reason as I entertained the conversation he had opened.

"Really? They asked you to coach? What did you say?" Was he interested in coaching again? I had thought that he didn't like coaching.

"I told them 'Thanks, but no thanks,'" my husband explained in his usual nonchalant tone. I listened for a hidden meaning behind his words and found none.

"Really? Are you happy with your decision?" I wondered if he was truly happy here in Vegas, teaching and lecturing. A tiny part of me wished he wasn't. I wished he was feeling the dissatisfaction that I was feeling; that he wanted to go back home. Okay, a giant part of me, all of me, really, wished that he were unhappy here.

"Yes. I didn't like coaching. It's not for me. Plus, I don't have the time. I travel too much with all the lectures that I do. And those will only multiply as time goes on." He smiled at me in a way that a father smiles at his eight-year-old child and patted my leg.

"You plan to do *more* lectures?" I realized that I officially didn't know my husband anymore. Apparently, he had no desire to know me either. My heart sank into my stomach, resting upon the unease that now churned there.

"Yes, I love it."

And you don't love me enough to want to be home so often.

Out loud, I told him, "I bet they were disappointed about your answer. You hold quite a few records in your division."

"*Held* a few records," he corrected me.

"You still have one that hasn't been beat."

"Well, I think they'll be okay. I gave them someone who is just as good at coaching as they are at swimming." Craig grinned.

"Oh really? Who's that?"

He patted my knee and grinned even wider. I wanted to turn my head to see the eight-year-old that had to have been standing behind my shoulder. But, my logic knew better. He was smiling like that at me.

"Oh no!" I said, "I can't do it. It's a Men's swim team. I'm a woman. That's - that's - that's preposterous! Did they laugh hysterically when you gave them my name?"

"No. I told them about how I coached for a bit at Penn, while Clemens was on sabbatical. And, I told them how I was no good at it. Then, I explained to them how you stepped up and helped me out and basically coached the men for me until Clemens returned. You were really something else. Those boys looked up to you."

I was taken aback. I couldn't believe that Craig held me in such esteem! Never, had I thought that any of the coaching help I had given him in the past had ever meant anything to Craig. He certainly never gave me any "atta girl's" at the time. That was a tough year for him, though. It was hard on his ego to admit that he was no good at coaching. Swimming was a sport that he was passionate about.

"Anyway," Craig continued, "I told them that you would be stoked to accept the position. The job is yours." Craig turned off the car, proud of himself. He gave me a kiss on the cheek, as if to say, "You're welcome, Toots!"

We were in front of the widow's house now.

"What?" I couldn't quite process all this. It was terrifying to think that someone would just hand me a team like that. Some of the guys on the team were actually planning on going to the next Olympics! That was a lot of pressure to put on one person.

My eyes bugged out of my head. My voice rose an octave, "You didn't even ask me! What if I don't want to do it?"

My initial shock had turned into abhorrence. Was Craig out of his mind? Did he actually think that I wanted to be the only female men's swim coach in the Mountain West Conference? It was embarrassing. I couldn't even go into the team's locker room.

"Why wouldn't you want to do it?" he asked, a trace of annoyance in his voice.

"Well, it's an overwhelmingly large task. Why don't they ask the assistant coach to do it?"

"He quit."

"What? You mean I'd be brand new and all alone?" *Were the powers that be at UNLV's athletic department insane? Who okayed this?* I wondered, still feeling blind-sided by the idea of coaching in general.

"They'll find another assistant coach. Susan, this is an opportunity of a lifetime. I would jump at it if I could."

"Yes, but you could jump and you didn't. And I'm not you. I don't want to jump into the Runnin' Rebels Men's Swim Team. The only place I care to jump is into the water – alone. Or off a cliff. Yes, the cliff is sounding much better than coaching an all-male team."

"You're being overdramatic."

"And you're crazy if you think I will actually do it."

"Just think about it. Don't say 'yes' or 'no' yet." He patted my knee, "We need to go inside so we don't look like a couple fighting out here on the curb." He spoke to me in a condescending voice. *Was that imaginary eight-year-old still standing behind me?*

We got out of the car and Craig added, "Oh, and Susan, if any of the Athletic Directors in the house talk to you about taking over the team, just go with it, okay?"

That's when I lost it! My body temperature rose as I spouted off at him, "Oh my Fuck! Craig! I can't believe this....You cocky Son of a bitch!" I bubbled over with anger, hoping he would be offended by my choice of words.

He looked right through me, ignored my verbal lashing, took my hand and sauntered into the funeral after-party.

My anger quickly transformed into defeat as I realized that my words made no impact upon Craig. How silly he must have thought I was acting. My body went cold and my muscles tightened.

The second we stepped indoors, Craig was swept away by some old teammates from Penn (of course) and I wandered off on my own. I consciously forced my clenched jaw to relax and held my chin up. Surely, someone that I knew from Penn State would be visiting for the funeral too.

I waded through the sea of mourners and felt as though the eyes of the strangers were following me. Was I paranoid? I looked around and swore a guy from across the room pointed me out to someone else. Why would they be looking at me? Was my skirt caught on my underwear or something? I swept a hand across my rear and it was all clear. *What the heck was going on*?

Craig made eye contact with me through the crowd around him and smiled. He was still very handsome at his age – from twelve feet away. I smiled back and tried to mouth the words to him, "Do I have something on my face?"

He looked confused and mouthed back, "What?"

"Do I –" I began to mouth it again, slowly, when I was ambushed! She came out of nowhere; a bouncy, young, redheaded girl jumped into my site line. She was geared up to take me as her conversation hostage.

41

"Hi! I'm Kamber." She spoke enthusiastically and thrust out her hand. I shifted my body back to regain some of my personal space and grudgingly placed my hand in hers. She shook it vigorously, pulling my body toward her.

"Hi, Kamber. I'm Susan Templeton." I tried to match my vocal tone to Kamber's own, but was unsuccessful. Instead of sounding perky, I sounded sarcastic. Of course I was being *sarcastic*, but I didn't need Kamber to know that. Luckily, she was too into her own agenda to even notice my mockery.

"I know. You're the new men's swim coach, right?" She was all about getting the dish on me. How did the little vulture know about the coaching job when I had only learned the news, myself, five minutes ago?

"I, umm, I...I guess. Yes." Man, was I tongue-tied these days! I hadn't had enough time to think about it. Coaching a men's team at the collegiate level was the opportunity of a lifetime for me, but oh my gosh – It was the *mens' team*. I was missing the essential genitalia needed to fit in with that group! How would I do it? How would they accept me or even listen to me? For Craig's sake, I would go along with it today. But, come Monday I would step down.

Kamber stood in my space and gabbed on and on, speaking to me as if I were an old friend. Well, she was speaking *at me* anyway, but I barely heard her. My brain felt foggy and overwhelmed. It was a good thing that she didn't notice my lack of response to her rather meaningless words. But, then she said something that got my attention.

"So," she began to speak in a hushed tone, "Who do you think killed coach Sutton?" The cloud in my mind dissipated instantly.

"What?" I asked, flabbergasted by her audacity. I was finally listening to the little gossipy girl.

"I said," She spoke slower, still in a whisper, "Who do you think did it?"

"What do you mean? It was an accident. He died of food poisoning." I reasoned and wondered if Kamber had escaped from a mental institution.

"Did he?" She asked me in a tone that insinuated she knew something that I didn't.

"Yes. It could happen to anyone." I told her flatly, wishing I hadn't taken the bait.

"Could it?" She asked with more than a hint of skepticism. Boy did she have some nerve! If she wasn't batty, then she was the epitome of impudent. Who was this *Kamber* anyway?

"Yes. It was an accident, *Kamber*." I repeated, deciding that she had no excuse for this inappropriate behavior. *Kamber* was disrespectful and rude.

Her jaw dropped as I began to lay into her, "And I'd appreciate you not talking to me about my dead friend as if he's today's gossip. Clearly, you didn't know him! Clearly, you are some tag-along, here for the ride! Your words – Your accusations hurt those who are mourning!" I realized that I was starting to speak louder, so I lowered my voice and added, "Do not speak to me again. Good bye."

I walked away, disturbed by Kamber's offensiveness. What was up with her? I wandered outside, trying to figure out what would possess anyone to walk up to a perfect stranger and ask them, balls out, who they thought had killed their friend.

Sutton's widow was outside on the back porch. She stood alone, smoking a cigarette under the shade of her overhead decking. It was now or never. I approached her slowly. My heart fluttered, unsure how to react to the stress. All the words were seemingly erased from my vocabulary, as I tried to come up with an opening line.

Luckily, she heard the clack of my heels on the wood and turned to face me. "Susan," she faked a smile and gave me a light hug.

"Elizabeth," I said her name as gingerly as the hug she gave me. Her body felt frail under my embrace. I didn't want to break her. One wrong word from me and she would be damaged beyond repair. *The poor thing!* Her heart was broken. Her former life was lost. She would never be the same. Her eyes told it all; they were well aware her current situation. Elizabeth had lost everything.

"I'm so sorry," I told her. My eyes felt wet. *Don't cry,* I told myself. I could feel the sting in my nose. *My God, Susan! Do not cry! This is her time to mourn! Your job is to support her, not to make it worse! Don't cry! Don't cry! Don't cry!*

I didn't cry. It almost happened, but I caught myself. I gulped down a large breath of air. It tasted like tobacco and tar, mixed with wet grass.

"Yes," the widow muttered. She took a deep inhale of her cigarette. "Want a smoke?" she asked.

I didn't want to be rude, but the smell of cigarette smoke was making me dizzy, so I declined her offer.

"It's so weird." Elizabeth spoke to no one in particular, "I keep expecting him to come out here. We used to sit on the deck and look out at the Vegas Valley. We'd watch the sun set. He rubbed my feet." She began to cry. Tears raced down her cheeks. She took another puff between sobs. Her cigarette was moist, but she didn't notice. Between sobs and puffs, she continued to speak, "He rubbed my feet all the time," Puff, sob, puff, "And I never," Puff, sob, "Rubbed his." She sobbed and puffed some more.

I had no idea what to do. Her face and cigarette were covered in tears. I didn't really want to hug her. She was such a mess and I didn't think she wanted me, a mere acquaintance, to console her. I placed a hesitant hand on her shoulder. She shivered and walked to the other end of the deck. *Point taken.*

I said nothing else. Turning on my heels, I just headed back indoors.

I stepped inside through the sliding door and there stood my student. His body was facing mine from a foot away. I hadn't noticed him there through the glass. Todd was just about to cross to the outside.

"Hi, Todd," I said, still feeling weird and useless.

"Hi, Professor."

"It's Susan," I said, suddenly sick of the word "Professor." That was not who I was. That was my husband, the man who could do no wrong. I bet Craig would have known what to say to the grieving widow. I bet she wouldn't have shivered and walked away from him. He was a people person. Craig knew how to talk to people. And I was just me, just Susan. Susan crumbled under the pressure of face-to-face conversations during moments of stress. Susan spoke about herself in third person and then rolled her eyes sarcastically at her own thoughts.

"Susan?" Todd clarified straddling the doorway. I could feel the heat from his body.

"Just Susan," I told him. I felt exhausted and dizzy. Between the surprise coaching job, Kamber and Elizabeth, I was on sensory overload.

"No, not *just* Susan." Todd corrected me. It was so cute. He was trying to cheer me up. He reminded me a lot of Craig when he was younger, in that boyishly handsome sort of way.

"No?" I pretended to be intrigued.

"Susan, the teacher," He began, "Susan, the Coach." I rolled my eyes at this and took a step inside the door, attempting to create more distance between our bodies.

He took my hands in his, "Susan, my friend." Todd gave my hands a light squeeze and let go. I noticed how soft his skin was.

"Thanks," I said, embarrassed that my student had witnessed my weak moment. "I see someone I must say 'hi' to," I pretended to make eye contact with a lady I didn't know. "I'll catch up with you later." I gave his shoulder a small pat and rushed away.

When I got across to the Lady I didn't know, I had no idea if Todd was still watching, so I had to keep up the charade. "Hi," I said to her and gave her a fake hug. She smelled of gin and lavender.

The lady I hugged returned the fake smile and cooed, "Hi," back to me. I couldn't believe she didn't sell me out! The lady didn't even flinch as she squeezed me back. Her embrace was much more emphatic than mine. Strangers must hug her often, I surmised.

"I'm sorry, Dear," she said to me, "I don't remember your name." I was impressed by her sincere eye contact and manners.

"I'm Susan Templeton."

"Oh!" She looked at me with recognition then, "The new coach!"

How did everyone know this already?

"Yes, apparently, I am." I couldn't say 'no' to the nice old lady. Plus, I had promised Craig, the man I loathed at the moment, that I would go along with it. "If you don't mind my asking, how did you know that I am the new swim coach?"

"I don't mind at all. My husband is the Athletic Director at the University, Mrs. Templeton." She glanced at a tan, weathered man drinking a brandy across the room and smiled.

That made sense. But, then, how did Kamber know the news? *Was the little old lady telling everyone my business?*

She must have read my mind because she added, "But, even if I weren't married to the Director, I would have found out soon enough. That youngin' over there has taken up residence as the town crier. If you ask me, she has no couth gossiping and asking all those questions right after a funeral." She gestured toward Kamber across the room, who could be seen pumping two swim team members for information at the same time.

The boys appeared bored by Kamber's intrusion and didn't look like they were giving up any information. I wished she would just stop it already. Not that I knew what "it" was.

"Yeah. She already got to me." I shared. "Who is she? Why is she here?"

"She's a journalist for the school newspaper. She also happens to be Coach Sutton's niece. Go figure."

"Go figure." I repeated as my eyes swept the room.

Two figures caught my attention through the sliding door. The widow, Elizabeth Sutton, leaned on the deck, just as she had when I found her outside earlier. The person next to her was Todd. He was standing very close, as though he were sharing a secret with her. I had no idea he was so close with his Coach's wife, now widow.

I wondered what he was saying to make her feel better. Whatever it was, Elizabeth appeared to be engaging his line of conversation with much more interest than she had taken in mine.

I realized I was staring at them and whipped my head in the opposite direction just as Todd broke away from the widow and walked to the sliding door.

I strode to the drink table and ladled some punch into the large serving spoon.

I tried to focus on pouring the drink and then on sipping the drink, but I couldn't stand it. Slowly, my eyes shifted to the side over the outer edge of my plastic cup. I could see nothing on my peripheral vision. I swallowed and turned my head to look in his direction. There he was; a tall, broad boy, who looked very manly in his suit and tie. I couldn't help but perve over him at that moment.

Did I feel guilty for having sexual thoughts about a student? *Yes.*

No.

Maybe...

Well, it didn't happen very often. It was a tough day, what with all the mourning and added stress of coaching an all male team. And Todd's face had that boyish charm. His crooked smile made me weak. Could anyone really blame me? He was sexy – especially in my fantasy – he was *sexy!* Besides, no one would ever know. The desire to touch my fingertips to his youthful cheek was locked up, deep inside of my mind.

5

I ground my chewing gum into my molars as I marched up the sidewalk leading to the University's fitness center. The grey building houses two basketball courts, the only pool on campus, a dojo and a zillion racquetball courts. I knew that I should spit the gum out, but somehow the pain in my jaw took away from the acid rising in my gut.

I was walking through the familiar haze of a bad dream destined to end in tragedy, unless I awoke. There was no way it was really happening. But it was. I was awake and moving through the hall that led to a new phase of my life and it was scary.

I was about to introduce myself to the swim team for the first time as their new coach. Why did I agree to this again? Oh yeah, that dumb ass, Craig, agreed to it for me and I didn't have the nerve to back out. Now, he was out of town, probably eating room service and jumping on the cushy bed in his hotel room.

He does a good job of milking those seminars he teaches. He manages to do very little actual speaking and quite a lot of recreation in the different cities he visits. But that's his thing. He loves people and they love him. They beg him to come speak for a few hours and implore him to indulge them in a round of golf before he leaves. I wish I had a little more of that people mojo that Craig possesses.

Alas, I am me. *I am all I have to offer those boys in there. I am a great swimmer and a good coach,* I told myself. Craig wasn't so good at coaching. *I can be proud and happy to be Coach Susan Templeton this morning,* I talked myself up in my mind.

I have a lot to offer. I have a lot to offer. I have a lot to offer. I repeated the mantra.

As I walked through the grey stone hallway, the sound of my shoes hitting the concrete floor ricocheted between my eardrums. My heart raced. I felt unprepared; unready; incapable. This was just in my head, though.

I had practiced all week. I said my opening speech as the new coach to Puddles, my cat, three times last night. My stopwatch and whistle hung around my neck, in lieu of a badge, on which I would have had "Bad Ass Coach" inscribed, were it a reasonable option. Pressing on, I touched the two pseudo-badges tethered around my neck and felt a twinge of reassurance. With each step the decorated lanyards bounced off my chest with a ker-clunk, ker-clunk. Nonetheless, the two necklaces were my credentials. They were my nonverbal cue to the team that I was in fact a real coach. *Whistle equals coach, people,* I wanted to tell them.

The familiar smell of chlorine calmed my nerves a bit as I crossed the threshold to the men's swim team territory. My knees felt weak as I walked toward the high dive. No one was there.

Oh shit! I thought.

I had left each member of the team a voice mail yesterday. My only instruction to them was to meet me at the high dive at six a.m. It appeared that this was going to be even harder a job than I had anticipated. Prior to this moment my biggest worry had been that they would ignore my coaching or one kid would mouth off and I'd have to put him in his place. I hadn't even considered that the whole team might mutiny and stand me up.

My heartbeat slowed as I steadied my breath. I decided to continue on to the high dive. I would wait there in case the boys were just running late or something.

I kicked off my sport sandals and sat on the side of the pool, dangling my legs in the water. The smell of the chlorine combined with the warm massage of the water gave me peace. I thought about the situation. It was what it was. All I could do was lead these swimmers to water...If they didn't show... Well, I did the best I could. At least I could do some laps to make myself feel better if I wanted.

The swimmer in the lane next to me swam in the direction of the wall where I sat. His freestyle was much more graceful and way faster than it should be for a mere novice swimming for exercise. My eyes locked on him. He stroked all the way to the wall and stopped next to me without turning back. He dunked down, slicked back his hair and popped up to lean on the wall.

"Coach," he greeted me, with neither enthusiasm, nor disdain.

"Hello," I responded. I was surprised as hell, but did not let on. I looked around. Almost every lane was occupied. In my irrational state of mind, I had failed to see what was right in front of me. The team was already in the pool.

One by one, the swimmers in each of the lanes came to the wall and greeted me as, "Coach."

"Okay," I began when the last guy arrived at my end of the pool, "I said to meet me by the diving board. I didn't tell you to start without me."

"Uh, Coach Sutton always expected us to get here at five-thirty to warm-up before he arrived at six," one of the guys said from four lanes down.

I didn't want to traumatize them by changing up their schedule too much. "Very well then," I said, "Come on over from your lanes. I don't want to yell."

"If it's all the same to you, Coach, we'd like to just get on with the drills this morning. I'm sure you have some sort of a speech prepared, but we already know what you will probably say and stuff."

I searched for the face that belonged to the voice. There he was, Todd. He was sitting on the side a few lanes over.

"Really?" I questioned them as a whole, looking from guy to guy to guy. They were all nodding in agreement. Most of them hadn't bothered to take off their goggles.

"Very well then," I began again slowly, "Let me see what I'm working with. I want to see two laps of each stroke." I conjured up some moxie and stood up, relieved not to have to give them my speech, which I would have nailed. "Start with freestyle, then butterfly, breaststroke and backstroke. We aren't going for speed right now. I am only looking at technique."

I blew the whistle. "Go!"

I stood at attention, as they began to swim away.

A little rusty and new as their Coach, I forgot to give specific instructions as to how I wanted them to begin. A few dove from the side and the rest of the team just pushed off from the wall. I made a mental note to be more precise at tomorrow's practice. Details are very important when you are coaching.

I could tell they didn't want fireworks or a ceremonial "changing of the coach" type dialogue. They wanted to show up and swim - and keep their scholarships. They didn't want to be inspired by me; I wasn't their *real* coach. I was just there to tell them what to do. That worked for me.

My eyes studied them as a whole group. They looked like a strong team overall, no charity case walk-ons like you see on some teams.

As I analyzed them individually, I could tell who the egomaniacs were right off the bat. Three guys in the lanes furthest from me raced one another, even though I specifically had said that we weren't going for speed in these drills. I would have to keep an eye on them. Young guys with big egos could be a challenge for a coach. One of them might even have to be made an example of if the ego-driven behavior kept up.

The two-hour practice seemed to go on and on and on. It was a good thing that I brought a clipboard with all the things I wanted to do this morning written down because my mind went blank in between each drill. Then, when I figured each thing out, I railed off the instructions so quickly that we ran out of things to do. Apparently, the nervous adrenaline I had been trying to push aside had won out.

At 7:45, I let them leave the pool early.

I watched as men popped out of the water. Not boys. Not students. But men. Their shoulders and back muscles bulged from the workout. Their skin glistened as water droplets trickled down the length of their bodies and landed on the pool deck.

My breath was quick and shallow. A moment passed before I realized that I my eyes lingered on the half-naked figures before me. My head jerked away and I flipped my hair to cover the blush that had crept into my cheeks.

"Don't forget to hit the weight room tonight," I reminded them, looking anywhere but directly at the countless abdominal muscles before me.

After a sea of "See ya tomorrow, Coach," from each of the boys, I took off my whistle and stopwatch and dove in to the newly vacated pool. The water was heaven to my body.

The morning had felt like a complete disaster. I didn't remember coaching feeling like this when I had helped Craig out at Penn. But, then, I didn't have any of the responsibility or pressure riding on my shoulders then. I could feel the pressure now, weighing me down. And, although the swim team acted like they barely noticed my existence, I was sure that I had let them down today.

So I swam. In the water, I was weightless. I started with freestyle. It has always been my favorite stroke. It's so pure, simple and efficient. After ten laps, I still hadn't rid myself of the beast, so I switched to butterfly. I was working hard, aggressively pushing my way forward. I would either find solace or drown trying. My heart pounded in my chest. But, my breath stayed steady. My lungs were efficient from years of training, as I powered through the water. After a zillion more laps, I had finally exhausted the stress and embarrassment out of me. I felt centered.

I did the backstroke as a cool down. From my upside down vantage point, I noticed that one of the boys was standing on the side of the pool. He was watching me. It was Todd. I swam over to the side and slicked my hair back.

"You're a good swimmer, Susan." He smiled that crooked grin that made him irresistible to a lonely broad, such as myself. I had never thought of myself as the type of woman who anyone would refer to as a "broad," but in that moment, I felt like one. Craig hadn't been home much and when he was, he didn't try *anything*. The magnitude of my dry spell culminated in this moment. I wished Todd's smile meant that he was attracted to me. I wished that I could compete with whatever hot tail he was getting in college.

My cheeks flushed in response to his attention.

"Thanks," I responded to his compliment about my swimming skills.

"Seriously, you're shit is off the hook." He looked mesmerized by me.

Were my eyes playing tricks on me?

He continued to beam, "You are a f'in great swimmer. If the guys could see you…" he trailed off.

"What? Could see me what?"

He didn't respond. So, I finished the thought for him. "If they could see what a great swimmer I am, they would gain some respect for me? Is that what you were getting at?"

He looked embarrassed. Was he embarrassed for me or for himself? "Maybe." He agreed with my statement.

I had hoped he would disagree with me and put my deepest fears to sleep. Instead, he proved me right. It was a good thing I had just swum so much. I felt like decking him, but I could barely move my arms.

I think he saw the fire in my eyes.

"Maybe it's better they don't see you swim, though. They might get intimidated." His smile shifted from the right edge of his mouth across to the left.

"You're right." I concurred, "I could race them, but I'd send them all to the locker room crying." I opened my mouth to laugh out loud at the thought, but what came out was a giggle. *I'm acting like a twit!*

"Yeah. Plus, if they saw what I saw, then they'd all want you."

I was taken aback. Did he just insinuate what I thought he did or was it my fantasy again?

"Want me?" I let out a chuckle. "Right," I said, so Todd wouldn't think that I thought he was hitting on me. I knew it was wishful thinking on my part.

"Why not? You are one hot number, Susan. I mean, you are pretty, generally speaking, but when I saw you swim… mmm!"

"Oh, geez." *He really was hitting on me!* I popped out of the water now. Admittedly, it felt good. My ego swelled in response to this attention. But, this conversation had to be stopped. The sweet, young boy was tempting me.

"What?" He asked in an innocent voice.

"You feel way too comfortable with me, Todd." I warned him as I went to pick up my necklaces.

"Yeah, I know." He smiled a wicked, super-crooked smile. I could see the dirty thoughts dancing in his eyes.

"No, you don't know. You think you are safe to say whatever you want to me. But, you're wrong. Just because I am your teacher and your coach... Just because I am married... You are not safe." I wasn't sure if he understood what I was trying to tell him. I wasn't sure if I even understood exactly what I was saying.

"I'm not safe, huh? I'll take my chances."

He fell in step next to me as I made my way to the Women's locker room. I was determined to stop this conversation. He had crossed the line. It was my responsibility as his coach – as his teacher, to prevent anything from happening.

I restrained from speaking as I gathered my thoughts. My head spun in bewilderment. It felt so good to hear a man say he wanted me. This was the wrong man, though.

"What, Coach? You're not talking to me now?" he asked.

"You crossed the line, Todd." My lips pursed back closed again.

"Why? Because I told you that you were hot?

I nodded, determined to stare at his forehead, rather than his smile. I had fantasies about that mouth of his last night. If they surfaced in my mind now, my face would surely turn crimson and give me away.

"I really don't see the problem with my stating the obvious. You are a sexy mama." He elbowed me in an attempt to lighten the mood.

My skin felt electric where he touched me.

What I wanted to do was pull him by the waist into the nearest storage room and give him a lesson or two. It made me feel desirable to be wanted by someone so young and off-limits. *But he is off-limits, Susan! You will never go there.* I reminded myself.

The loneliness and longing I'd been feeling had been sated by Todd's declaration of admiration for me. How long would his words suppress my appetite, I wondered. Would it be enough just to know that he wanted me without actually finding out what it would feel like to connect with him physically?

It would have to be! Being his teacher was bad enough. Now that I was his coach, fulfilling my fantasies about him was absolutely out of the question. Not, that it was necessarily *in the question* before. I was, of course, married; married to a man who recently forgot that I exist.

I turned away and abruptly walked into the Women's locker room without saying goodbye.

I rounded the corner to the semi-private changing room and slumped against the wall, sucking in a deep breath. A prolonged exhale slowly escaped my nostrils and I wondered what the hell was wrong with me.

6

"Puddles peed in my shoe," Craig reported to me, without looking up from his seat.

"It's good to see you, too," I replied, dropping my bag on the organizer in the entryway.

"I'm sorry, Susie," Craig replied as he stood up from the sofa. "I missed you. How are you?" I studied his face for a trace of insincerity, but found none. He was legit.

"I'm fine." I gave him a fake hug. "I'm tired and a bit stressed, but I'm fine."

I felt abandoned while Craig was out of town the past four days. That didn't really matter though, since lately I felt just as isolated when he was at home with me.

This was the first I'd seen of Craig since he'd been back in Vegas, and I couldn't make up my mind as to whether or not I missed him in his absence. He certainly didn't dominate my fantasies anymore. It had been more than a year since I had fantasized about my husband.

"How's coaching?" he asked.

"It sucks. I suck. I'm a suck-ass coach." Silently, I added, *And it's all your fault, Craig!* Everything was his fault. He gave *us* this horrid life in Vegas. But, it wasn't really *ours*. It was *his*. The life we made together was Craig's life. He had become a world traveler and I stayed home, coaching at his insistence. It was further proof that he was the star of *The Craig Show*. I was just the supporting cast.

"It's a transition period. Just remember that. It will get easier," he soothed, trying to put me at ease about being a new coach.

"Really? When?"

"I don't know. In time, I guess."

"Thanks." I rolled my eyes. I wished he could take the discomfort away with his few words, but he couldn't. The only person who could change how I felt about the whole coaching thing was me.

"You are a great coach, Susan. You'll get it right."

"Thanks," I muttered, picking up the cat. Puddles rubbed her cheek on my chin. She was my little angel. Yes, she peed on Craig's shoes, but it was only because he had it coming to him. "Good girl, Puddles," I whispered in her furry ear. She purred and pawed at me in response.

"I'm hungry. You want a sandwich?" Craig asked. He was so sweet sometimes. Craig wasn't the type to deep clean the house, but he helped out in other ways. I loved that he did little things for me, like taking the trash out and preparing meals. He even loaded the dishwasher from time to time, unasked.

"Sure, I'd love a sandwich." I put puddles down and followed Craig into the kitchen. Maybe I was overreacting to our Vegas situation. A sour sensation of guilt rose in my gut as I thought about the fact that I was married to a nice, attractive man whom I didn't appreciate.

I pulled on his shoulder and turned him to face me. He smiled a genuine smile. Placing my hand on the nape of his neck, I pulled him in for a kiss. I started softly and then I slowly slipped him the tongue. It felt good to kiss my husband the way I had been fantasizing about kissing other men. That is, it felt good until he pulled away. *Satisfaction denied!*

Craig slithered out of my arms and turned back to his sandwich. He took a bite as if it were the most natural thing in the world to turn away from seduction in favor of ham and cheese.

What the hell?

I was discouraged, embarrassed and hurt. The lust that had built up inside me during our kiss throbbed in my groin. Steam rose through my body, pushing at the small pores in my skin. My throat swelled as the horrified feeling of being rejected set in. I didn't know whether to scream or cry.

What a jerk-off! I screamed in my head. He was practically pushing me into the arms of another man!

I continued my silent rant that was so deafening in my head, I was sure Craig could hear it. *I'm not proud to admit it, but I need to feel wanted. I know I should love myself. And, I do. But loving myself is not enough for me. I need to feel wanted and loved by another being. Maybe needing to feel sought after is selfish, or immature, or it exposes my hidden insecurities. But, there it is. I need a man to want me in order to feel validated as a sexual being. That is the dirty truth.*

Craig was sweet and nice. He had what a French person would call, "je ne sais quoi." Everyone loved him. And he loved himself, too. Craig didn't need my love to feel validated. Maybe that was his problem. He assumed that I was just as secure as he was. At this point, I wasn't.

All I could do was accept the situation for what it was. I wanted sex and he didn't want it for reasons that were still unknown to me. The rational thing to do was to wait until Craig was ready to talk to me. He couldn't hold out on intercourse for much longer without offering up some sort of explanation.

I took in a mouthful of air. I could wait.

On the bright side, the sandwiches Craig made were worthy of a new pair of shoes to replace those that Puddles had ruined. I made a mental note to go shopping tomorrow.

We had an average evening for us. Reality television was followed by an hour of silent reading in bed and the big finish – drum roll please - rolling over and falling asleep; Craig's oppressive leg weighted across my body.

When he began to snore, I turned to thoughts about Todd, the one male in my life who did want me. I recalled his words from earlier and pictured us together in my mind. This time I came up with an alternate ending to our conversation. When he elbowed me in jest, I swung around, whipping my hair with me, and pulled him close.

I shoved Craig's leg off of me. He snarled what must have been a snore loud enough for the neighbors to hear, but he didn't wake up. My body, now free from the weight of my husband, longed to be touched. I lifted my index finger to my mouth and moistened it with my tongue. I rolled to my back and spread my legs. My fingertips moved down the space I had created and made soft circles around the sensitive skin. I felt blood rush to my lips in response.

I pressed at my clit and opened my mouth, letting out a muted moan. My index finger slid inside of myself and arched my back, imagining that it was Todd inside of me. It felt wet and warm. Silently, I pleasured myself.

I pictured Todd's crooked smile as plain as if he were on top of me right there, in the bed next to Craig. Hot and flushed, I added more fingers and feverishly pushed in and out. My pussy swelled and pulsed.

I pressed down onto my favorite sweet spot and let everything go. A tiny squeal escaped from my mouth as my back collapsed back onto the bed. I quickly covered my red face with a pillow.

"You okay?" Craig grunted without even opening his eyes.

"Yes. Just pleasuring myself," I whispered, titillated by my independent act of indecency and thrilled at the aspect of getting caught. Maybe knowing that I was touching myself would arouse him.

"Oh," he replied and rolled over with a snort.

What a buzz kill! He couldn't care less that I was horny and masturbating in the bed next to him. My heart sank.

In that moment I realized that I could have invited the entire swim team over for a gang bang and Craig would have slept soundly through it all, in his ignorant, uncaring bliss.

I   hated   him!

And I loathed myself for not doing anything about the rut we were stuck in.

*****

"Coach," Todd approached me after practice.

"Yes?" I knew what he was going to say. Any guy forced to be around a woman he had hit on shamelessly, and unsuccessfully, would try and smooth things over to keep the peace. Young guys have no idea how transparent they are.

"I'm sorry about my behavior yesterday, aight? It was a straight dis. You are my coach and my teacher and I can respect that."

"It's okay, Todd." I blushed, remembering last night's fantasy. Now, I regretted having turned him down. What if I never got another chance to fool around with a hot, young male in real life?

No! No way, I thought, *I am not going to keep on letting life just happen around me, while I sit by idly, feeling discontented in the background.*

I patted the side of his arm and continued, "Perhaps I overacted. I'm actually flattered that you think that way about me."

He smiled his crooked smile. "You're, uh, flattered?"

"Yes, Todd. I am flattered. I'm sorry if I was a bit curt with you yesterday. I didn't want to give you the wrong idea, or worse, lose your respect as your coach." I steadied my breath in an attempt to soften the redness I felt warming my cheeks.

"Okay, I follow. You're flattered, but you're not surprised or interested because you get hit on all the time, right?"

"What?"

"I imagine that a lot of your students like you in that way," Todd explained.

"No. Actually, you're my first." I couldn't believe that we were talking about this.

"Really? I don't buy that for a second. All the young Romeos want you."

"Well, you're the first student who over told me, anyway."

"I bet the playas think about you when they're in the shower," Todd teased me.

"You're crazy. They think of me as an old lady. Young boys think about *young girls* in the shower."

"What about Mrs. Robinson?"

"She went after him, not, vice versa. *She* chased the Dustin Hoffman character," I told my young admirer. "What was his name?"

"Whose name"

"The guy in *The Graduate*? Dustin Hoffman's character?"

"Who cares?" Todd said flippantly. He touched my hair. My scalp tingled. It felt *so good!* I wanted him to do it again, but he didn't. He stepped back and looked me up and down with that silly lopsided grin that made my knees go weak.

I felt both elated and horrible at once. It was nonsensical. What was going on inside me that would ever possess me to interact with a man-child in such a way? But, damn, it felt good!

"Wanna walk me to my next class?" he asked.

That seemed innocent enough.

"Sure. I'll meet you outside the locker rooms." I couldn't believe I was doing this. I was fraternizing with members the team. A coach fraternizing with members whom she finds attractive; it was sketchy at the very least.

"So, Mrs. Templeton," Todd crooned as we walked under the hot Vegas sun, "You've never messed around with a student?"

I wasn't sure, but I was beginning to think that Todd was more interested in getting it on with an older chic, than he was into getting it on with Susan Templeton.

What am I doing? I silently scolded myself for being so stupid. *Walking him to class? Seriously, Susan!*

"No, Todd." I looked straight ahead as I answered, "I have never messed around with a student."

My face was pursed into an expressionless veneer. I tried with all my strength not to look at him.

"Have you ever been attracted to a student?" I felt his eyes study my face.

"I have thought that students were good looking before, yes." I made the mistake of looking at him. He caught me. I quickly turned my gaze forward again.

"Oh, I thought I was your first."

"Get over yourself, Todd." I tried to downplay the situation. I wanted to make him feel less thrilled with himself.

"Ouch," he said, finally staring blankly ahead, as I did. We walked across campus in silence for a few minutes. I said hi to a colleague of Craig's as he paced past us quickly.

Todd said hello to a few friends of his as we passed by the library.

I didn't worry about being seen with Todd on campus. It was not unusual for students to walk and talk with their teachers. My face was stoic. And, it wasn't like we were holding hands or anything.

We cut though the cactus garden, where we found a bit of shade for our journey. The desert landscape was sparely decorated. It was just the plants, a few benches, this boy and me. The smell of red dirt and sage danced in my nostrils.

Todd broke the silence. I could tell that he didn't want to leave the garden just yet. "Have you ever cheated on your husband?" he asked.

"No," I replied.

"Oh." He stopped in front of a bench and asked me, "You wanna to sit for a sec?"

"I thought you were going to class. Do you have time to, uh, sit?"

"I got a few minutes to spare." There was that boyish, crooked smile again. His eyes lit up. It was impossible to resist.

"Okay." We sat on a bench, next to a small waterfall coming out of a clay pot. A tree blocked us from the view of any passersby on the main trail.

"What's your husband like?" Todd asked.

"Why do you want to know?"

"I think you like me, Susan. I want to know why. Does he treat you bad? Is he mean? Does he have a temper?"

"No. He is very nice. He treats me with kindness. Everyone likes him." I was honest with Todd. I wasn't going to feed him some bullshit about Craig being mean to me just so that he could feel better about his own feelings. The truth was that my husband was a nice guy. I simply resented him because he took me from my home in Pennsylvania and then stopped giving me what I needed once we settled in our new house here. That was not Todd's business.

"Huh." Todd mulled this over for a moment, "So he's a nice guy…" He leaned in. "So if I kissed you, I'd be kissing the wife of a nice guy? A guy that everybody likes?" He touched the inside of my palm with his finger. Goosebumps rose on my flesh, an involuntary response to his feather-like touch.

"Yes. I'm not making excuses for you or for me," I told him.

"That sucks, because I really want to kiss you."

"I like that you want to kiss me," I goaded him. The attention Todd paid to me fed the hungry part of my psyche. It was as if I hadn't eaten in a month and my stomach had grown smaller, but now that he gave me a taste of an appetizer, I was ravenous for more sustenance. I loved this admiration and I wanted to hear him tell me more of his adoring thoughts.

"Come on, Susan. You have to give me something to go on. Do you like me too or will it be awkward the next time I see you again? It was weird at practice today."

That was a tough request. He wanted me to reciprocate. I never wanted to admit my secret feelings about this youthful and handsome student on the swim team that I coached. A week ago, I could not have predicted that I would actually live out one of my secret desires. It wasn't against the law to be with him. He was an adult. But, ethically, as his teacher and as his coach, I would be crossing some huge boundaries if I gave into his request and gave him the green light.

"You are an excellent swimmer," I began, finding difficulty voicing what I was feeling out loud. "I think that you are a good student, too. I can tell that you study. Speech is not your best subject, but you work very hard."

"Aight. Time to bounce. I gotta get going to class," Todd said. He didn't try to mask the disappointment in his voice.

I wanted to tell him how sexy he was. I wanted to take him and kiss him and feel him up, but I couldn't get past the incredible guilt I was having for even thinking about it. I imagined that the guilt would only intensify if I were to actually act upon my fantasies. *Why couldn't he just fawn over me while I feigned indifference?*

"Okay," I told him, readying myself to let him walk away. But, my body had a different plan for me. As he stood up, I grabbed his hand and pulled him back to the bench. I spread my fingers and intertwined them with his. I placed a hand on his face, pulling him to me. I gave him a longing glance and watched him smile. My heart melted. I returned his smile and laid one on him.

I kissed him hard. There was no tenderness between our lips. He kissed me back. His tongue was large in my mouth and I loved how it filled me up. Todd's arms wrapped around my waist and he pulled me close to him. I felt my breast press on his chest. We continued to feel each other's mouths with our tongues until we finally parted for air. I could taste the sage as I sucked down a deep breath of desert air.

Todd looked at me wildly. I had confused the heck out him. *Well done, Templeton*, I thought sarcastically. I was going to screw this kid up for all future girlfriends.

"I guess I do like you," I said, as if to confirm out loud what I had just done. I couldn't control the smile that camped out on my face. My brain danced in my head. I was high on pleasure.

Todd's face relaxed and he gave me a small lopsided smile. "I like that you like me." Without missing a beat, he wrinkled his forehead and admitted, "I really do have to get to class now."

"See you at practice," I waved, still lightheaded and giddy. I sat alone on the bench and watched him dash off.

7

The Fashion Show Mall on the Vegas strip was uncharacteristically busy for a Thursday. Although the gobs of people, mostly tourists, bothered me, I was glad to see that the mall was getting so much business. It was a sign that the economy was doing better.

My first stop was the coffee shop in front of Nordstrom. I would need some caffeine to survive the mall. The first sip of my latte was luscious. I took a deep inhale, tasting the rich flavor of espresso that lingered on my tongue. Satisfied that the best drink ever invented would make this experience palatable, I turned to leave.

That was a mistake!

I walked out of the coffee shop and before I could duck behind a trashcan, I spotted a familiar face, leering through the crowd of tourists under a bouncy coif of red hair.

I looked down at the tiled floor and began to walk in the opposite direction at a quick pace. Maybe she wouldn't notice me.

"Coach!" *Damnit all to Hell!* She saw me. I was trapped. There was no chance of pretending not to see her there.

"Hi, Kamber." I hoped that her journalistic instincts couldn't sniff out my irritation. Not many people got under my skin, but this *Kamber* girl sure left a foul taste in my mouth after Sutton's funeral. I would have been content having never spoken with her again.

The redhead sized me up in an obvious manner. "Hello," she spoke, "What are you up to today? Getting out of the heat?"

"No, I'm shopping. But, yes, the air conditioning is a bonus. And you, *Kamber*?" I tried to smile through gritted teeth.

"I'm looking for a gift for my boyfriend. It's his birthday."

"Great. Well, it was nice to see you," I said, pleased at the opportunity to walk away unscathed.

"Wait," Kamber pleaded with me, "Where are you headed? Let's walk together."

Oh, geez! I was too nice to say no. So, I told her the truth, "I'm on my way to the men's section in Nordstrom."

"Perfect! What are you looking for?" she asked as she matched my pace.

"Shoes for my husband. My cat peed in his shoes."

"Both of them? Gross." Kamber observed, as if it made difference if Puddles had only sullied one of his loafers, rather than both. Shopping with her wasn't so bad, so far. She hadn't grilled me for any information yet.

"Yes. It is gross. That's why I am replacing the shoes. What are you going to buy your boyfriend?"

"I don't know. Maybe a shirt."

"That's practical."

"Yeah. So, have you noticed anything odd at practice?" *So much for not being grilled.*

"Odd?" I tried to keep my tone light, but my stomach began to churn.

"Yes. There are twenty possible people who could have killed my uncle. No one is taking his death seriously, but I am."

"Perhaps, no one is looking for a killer because there is no killer. It was an accident, *Kamber*. It was food poisoning. Something Sutton ate didn't agree with his body. He got sick and passed away." Those last two words, I had to force out of my lips. I glared at her.

"I don't believe that for an instant," she said as if she were queen of all facts and figures.

"I'm guessing that you have a theory." I decided to hear Kamber's version of *who done it*. She was dead-set on telling me anyway.

"Yes," she began, "Sutton's wife did not want an autopsy. Obviously, she killed him," Kamber paused, then she added, overdramatically, "or her *lover* killed him."

I swallowed a huge gulp of my latte. "Her lover?" If that were true, then the lover must have been at the dinner party.

Was Sutton's wife screwing the swim team? *My* swim team? I went through a mental list of the roster. Which of the twenty fine young men on *my* team might she go for? I felt like a possessive mother - a possessive mother who had French-kissed one of her boys that morning. Okay, the thought of the mother analogy creeped me out. In my mind, I replaced the word, 'mother,' with the word, 'guardian.'

It didn't help.

Kamber, looked at me as if I were a silly little lamb. "You didn't know? Even Sutton had his suspicions."

"No. I didn't know. Of course I didn't know. How could I? And I doubt there's any truth to your theory. Anyway, how did you find out?" I asked her.

"I'm a journalist. I find everything out." Her face got all crinkly when she boasted.

"Really? You really find out everything? What do you know about me?" It was a test. I needed to know how good of a reporter she was.

"You didn't want to coach the men's swim team, but you took the job anyway."

"Please," I rolled my eyes.

"You did it because you didn't want to disappoint your husband."

I shot her another very ineffective eye roll.

"You hate Las Vegas and, although you want to make Mr. Professor happy, you do not like your husband very much." Kamber was trying to impress me with her ballsy talk.

She was good, but not that good. I wasn't going to let her get under my skin.

Kamber didn't know that I recently kissed an undergrad, or she would have sung to the skies about getting the scoop on that too.

A better reporter would have known that I was days away from sleeping with one of those guys whom she suspects of murder. She was just a nosy college kid who worked on the school newspaper.

"So, let me get this straight. You think that your aunt killed your uncle?" The idea was laughable.

"No. She didn't do it."

I gave her a questioning look.

"I think that she talked her lover into doing it," Kamber explained.

That was a horrendous lie! I was angry. "She looked pretty broken up at the funeral," I hissed.

"Wouldn't you be once the deed had actually been done? Planning to get rid of someone is much easier to deal with than their actual passing," she reasoned.

"Then who was her lover?"

"Someone on the swim team." As Kamber said it, she twirled her hair. It turned my stomach.

"How can you be so sure? Couldn't it have been someone else?"

"Yes, it could be someone else. But that doesn't make sense. The team was there that night."

She had a point there. I mean, had I chosen to believe her farfetched story, then it would make sense that the lover was at the house at the time when Sutton was poisoned.

"Okay, I'll go with that theory for now. Which of my boys was her lover?" I didn't take Kamber seriously, but it could come in handy to know whom on the team she thought was a psychotic killer.

"Well, since you asked. I have it narrowed down. There is Doug," she began.

"Doug?" I laughed. He was the skinniest kid on the team and a bit of a bookworm. Doug only swam for the scholarship. He was a bullet in the water, but not much to speak of outside of the pool.

"He's too quiet. I don't trust him." Kamber justified her logic. "It could also be Mike, Daniel, Dave or John."

"So, it could be anyone" I sighed, "Sounds like you need a new hobby. You're not getting anywhere with this." I did not need Kamber snooping around my team. What if she found out about my planned infidelity? I pondered the notion of keeping my distance from Todd for a while, but that didn't sound like very much fun. Ever since I had crossed the boundary by kissing Todd, the rest of the social no-no's didn't seem as important to me.

"I don't need a new hobby." Kamber was clearly offended. "I have narrowed the list down from twenty suspects to five persons of interest."

Gosh, she was an ass! Why was I talking to *Kamber* anyway? I picked up the pace of my steps through the bright store. Maybe she wouldn't be able to keep up with me.

I couldn't stand it, though; I had to ask her. I slowed back down and tried to sound detached.

"Really? Five sounds like a lot. Anyway, what disqualified the other guys from being 'persons of interest?' Why not someone like...like, uh, what's his name? Todd."

Kamber laughed like a rabid redheaded chipmunk. "Todd?" She snorted and giggled some more. "Yeah, that would be some cruel irony. The journalist's boyfriend turns out to be the killer. Life isn't that cruel."

Oh shit!

Did I hear that correctly? Todd was Kamber's boyfriend? She was his...

Yuck!

I had to go wash my mouth out. This was horrid! The cheating on my husband thing I could handle. The fooling around with a student I coached, I had gotten past. But, this – this was wretched! I had kissed the mouth of the person who slept with the most annoying girl on campus!

A bit of sour tasting vomit rose up into my mouth.

"You'd be surprised at how cruel life can be," I said as I swallowed it back down – my punishment for trying to add some pleasure and excitement to my life.

I was dying for mouthwash. Promptly, I paid for a pair of shoes that looked like the twins of those that Puddles had sullied.

"Man, you are bitter," Kamber observed in her forward, pompous manner.

"You have no idea," I told her, dying to break free. I thrust my hand into hers and shook it, before throwing it back at her. "This has been fabulous, but I have to go."

I turned around, storming toward the exit.

"Coach?" Kamber called from my dust.

I ignored her.

"Coach!" She screeched.

A store clerk looked at me funny, so I slowed to a stop and turned to face her, now three hundred feet away.

Kamber held up a Nordstrom bag. "Shoes?"

"Right." I strutted over, my chin pointed up and snatched the bag from her fingertips.

"Take care of yourself, Coach. You look a bit pale," she told me as if she cared.

*****

I placed Craig's new shoes in his closet and began to make dinner. Cooking was out of character for me, but I was feeling like such a schmuck for kissing Todd. Perhaps, I could erase that memory from my mind and chalk it up to a mistake. Craig and I could rekindle things and I would once again feel satisfied at home.

My cell phone buzzed on the countertop. I picked it up to see a text.

HEY SEXy. WAT R U DOIN?

It was from Todd. I decided not to reply in favor of cutting up the carrots.

The lock on the front door made a sound. Puddles meowed. "Yes, your Daddy's home," I told her. "I'm in the kitchen," I called out to him, hoping that my voice sounded sweet and alluring, rather than vile and adulterous.

Craig came in and I watched him smile. "What did you do?" he joked, viewing my not-so-Susan-esque behavior. If he only knew the truth behind his observation... *Would he leave me?* I wondered, surprised that the thought of Craig leaving scared me.

I made out with a student. I told him with my eyes. *He was young and hot and his dick got hard just from kissing.*

Craig was not a mind reader. He barely heard me when I spoke out loud. He would never know what I was thinking, or what I had been up to, unless I told him. Even then, it was a fifty-fifty shot that he would actually hear what I said.

He kissed my forehead and picked up a knife. "What can I do?" he asked, sharpening the tool on a block. He loved that knife. Craig loved all things sharp. His favorite Christmas present was a samurai sword that I never let him hang on the wall.

"You can slice that onion." I told him as my phone buzzed again. I snatched it up before he could see whom the text was from.

DID U GET MY TXT? I MISS U, SEXY.

I hit "delete" and put the phone down. Craig didn't notice that I had turned red. He was fighting tears from the onion.

"How was your day?" I asked my husband.

"It was great – very fulfilling," Craig said with a hint of sarcasm.

"Fulfilling, eh? Well, that is just awesome. Puddles bought you some new shoes." I gestured down to the furry little beast on the floor between my ankles.

"Thanks, Puddles," he said to the cat and dropped a piece of chicken into her bowl. She meowed, sauntered over and lazily licked at the meat.

My phone buzzed again. Annoyance filled my thoughts. *Son of a bitch!*

I WANT 2 C U. CAN U GET AWAY 2NITE?

Craig was putting all the ingredients into the salad bowl. I decided that I had to text Todd back and stop the texting insanity.

NO. STOP TXTING. WITH HUSBAND!

I hit the "send" button and put the phone in my pocket. Craig finally noticed that I was flustered. If only I were a better actor!

I took a breath. *Get it together!* I told myself, *Craig does not need to know about Todd. It will only hurt him. Be a better actor! Be the best!*

"Who keeps texting you?" he asked, sliding a tomato wedge into his mouth.

"Just a kid on the team. He wants to miss practice. I told him no. he got mad." Okay. That was a good lie. I studied Craig's reaction. He looked to be buying my line of crap.

Yes, I believed he bought it. I was a terribly good liar!

But, I had to change the subject, just in case. So, I began, "Did you hear that Coach Sutton's wife has a secret boyfriend on the side?"

That got Craig's attention. He choked on the tomato he had just taken a bite of.

After a few hard coughs, he was able to speak.

"What?" he managed to ask once he had cleared out his windpipe. His face was sweaty.

"Elizabeth Sutton has or had… I'm not sure which… a boy toy." I told Craig the juicy gossip.

"Do you need help? Are you okay, Craig?" I walked toward him.

"No, I'm fine." He stepped around the counter, grabbed a towel and wiped his face with it. "Who, uh, who was it?" he asked, his eyes peering above the towel.

"I don't know. I guess it was a member of the swim team."

"Oh," he said. The phone rang and Craig jumped to get it.

"It's for you," he told me, "It's Todd."

"Oh, thanks," I replied, slowly, keeping my heartbeat in check. *Damnit! What have I gotten myself into? Can't this kid take a hint?*

"Hi, Todd," I said in my most normal voice. I took the call right there in the kitchen. I didn't want Craig to suspect anything.

"Hi, Susan. It's Todd," Todd said.

"Yes. I know."

"I want to see you."

"I already told you 'no', Todd. No, you cannot miss practice tomorrow." I looked over at Craig who sat on a bar stool, eating the salad we had just made and looking through a science magazine. Apparently, his earlier attention had been short-lived. He was deep into the Craig Show now.

I probably could have had phone sex with Todd right there and my husband wouldn't have noticed. He had seemed more interested in the gossip about Elizabeth Sutton, than he appeared to be about my half of the phone conversation with Todd.

"I want to finish what we started today. You are so hot, Susan. I want you," he pleaded with me.

"That is very kind, Todd. But, I'm afraid that I cannot allow it. The entire team must go to practice everyday."

"I need you, Susan. I love you," he said.

Awe great! He's a psycho. I kissed a freakin' crazy kid!

"What? Todd, we can talk at practice tomorrow. I'm sure that this will pass. You will be okay."

"Come on!"

"Okay. I'll see you tomorrow."

"No."

"Yes. Make sure you are there."

"No! No! No!"

"Okay, Todd. Bye bye."

"Susan!"

I hung up the phone and tried to keep my breath steady. What was that anyway? *I love you?* Oh, he had better not love me!

"Kids," I rolled my eyes toward my husband.

Craig grunted in reply. He didn't even look up once to see my Academy Award worthy phone performance! I did not interest him. Why were we still married?

*****

Todd was early to practice Friday. He saw me in the hallway and ran toward me and picked me up. This action, of course, mad me hot with annoyance.

"Good morning, Susan!" He said with too much exuberance.

"Good morning, Todd. Please put me down." He put me down and I proceeded to lay into him. "What are you thinking!" I began to scold him, speaking at a fast pace, "We are in a public place. I am your coach and your teacher! I am married! We can't just be all chummy in public. This is not right! Your behavior is bad. Very bad! Do you understand?" I yelled at him in hushed tones.

"I'm sorry. I was just so excited to see you. I love you, Susan!"

"Stop, Todd! Stop! You do not love me!"

"Yes, I do!"

"No, you don't! I am just a fling – a crush." I reached out to his shoulders and gave him a shake, before releasing him quickly.

"How do you know?" he demanded.

"Well, you have a girlfriend, for one thing."

"Yes, and you have a husband, so what?"

"I told you that I am married. You didn't tell me that *Kamber* was your girlfriend."

"You didn't ask. And why do you say her name like that? *Kamber?* She is a nice girl." Todd wanted me to like her. He wanted me to approve of his slimy little wannabe reporter girlfriend. The boy had quite a few screws loose.

"She is not nice. She is a nosey know-it-all."

"Dude! That's rude."

"That's how I feel."

"Are you jealous of her? Is that what this is?" He put his arms around me and nuzzled his nose into my cheek. I wriggled away.

"No, I'm not jealous. I am so turned off!" I shivered at the thought of being under the spell of Todd only twenty-four hours ago. Now, I was relieved that it was broken. How could I have behaved so recklessly with someone so screwy?

"Do you want me to break up with her?" Todd kissed me lightly on the lips. It was a nice kiss. But, it was too late. It felt icky and wrong, rather than sexy and intriguing. The vomit from yesterday rose again in my throat.

"No," I told Todd, forcing the acid down my throat, "you should be with her, not me. I'm your coach. And I'm too busy to answer your text messages and too married to just visit with you and make-out at your whim. Besides, *Kamber* just bought you a shirt for your birthday. You deserve that shirt." I hoped that he didn't notice the sarcasm of the shirt comment. As his coach, I needed to break this off amicably. I didn't want to get a slew of nasty texts on my phone, or worse.

"Really, Coach," he paused to look at me, "*Kamber?*"

"Yes, Todd. You two belong together." I was done with him. He was boyishly handsome, but his choice of girlfriends and his over usage of the phone killed it for me. I couldn't cheat on my husband with a guy who was going to text me and call me at all hours. We had barely kissed and Todd was displaying stalker-like behavior. That wasn't my idea of fun.

He stared at the wall for a minute.

"Okay," He finally said.

I sighed in relief. *Phew! Stalker crisis diverted.*

"Okay. I'll see you at practice." I smacked his butt and sent him on his way to the locker room.

TOOT! I blew the whistle a zillion times at practice that morning.

"Andrew, come over here!" I barked.

The guys tolerated my presence, but they didn't exactly listen to me. At previous practices, I'd always felt that I at least had Todd on my side. But, since our chat this morning, he has become an anti-Coach-Templetonite, just like the rest of them.

I had had enough of their insubordination. The team would do as I said or they would have to swim elsewhere.

"Andrew, I showed you a better way to hold your hand while you swim. I showed it to you Monday! I showed it again on Wednesday and, then, again yesterday. What's it going to take to get you to do it right?"

Yes, I was in a bitchy mood. I knew that. They knew it, too. So what?

"I don't know what you're talking about, Coach."

"Your hand, Andrew. Your hand!" I yelled. Other swimmers looked over from their lanes. I stared down their curious eyes, like a wild cat guarding its prey from other animals.

"What are you guys looking at? Keep swimming. I'll call you over if I want to talk to you," I growled at the team. They quickly looked away and went back to their laps - sort of.

"What a bitch," Andrew muttered under his breath.

"What did you say?" My temper flared! My life was shit and I was taking it out on him. I deserved to be called a bitch, but not in front of the team. And not today! He wasn't getting out of the PE complex safely.

"I said, 'What a bitch.'" Andrew repeated with a casual smile, obviously proud of himself for talking back to me.

I couldn't believe what an idiot this jerk was. He was a college athlete. I was one of his superiors. All I had to do was kick him off the team and he would lose a scholarship worth sixty grand a year.

"Bitch? That's what I am, eh?"

"Yeah, Coach."

"You know what, Andrew. You can take your cocky attitude and enlarged ego and get the fuck out of this pool." He would just have to be an example to the others.

"What?" His smile faded.

I don't think Andrew expected this from me. He was one of our fastest swimmers and he wanted me to bow down to him. It wasn't going to happen. I was going to sacrifice the golden boy to get the rest of the team to listen to me.

By now the whole team had stopped swimming. The young men looked on in disbelief from their lanes as Andrew climbed out of the pool. His face set into a tight scowl.

"Bitch!" he said to my face and turned to walk away.

"I'm the Coach, you arrogant asshole!" I said to his back. "Don't come back, either, you rude ass son of a bitch! You are so fucking done here. I'm the Coach, Goddamn you!"

He gave me the finger over his shoulder and left.

I watched him leave.

I slowly turned to look at the sea of eyes in the pool. They all watched to see what I would do next. "I guess we're done for today," I told them, steaming from the fight with Andrew. At least one jerk was off the team. I hoped to God that the rest of the boys on the team would take this as their warning and start giving me a bit of respect.

The guys looked bewildered. No one spoke out loud as the group shuffled away to the locker room. I walked to the lifeguard office to grab a drink of water. Perhaps there would be something there I could throw at a wall. I gulped back the water, eyeing a stapler, when I heard a low voice.

"Coach?" I looked up to see one of the swimmers there. He was tall, dark, broad and brooding. I couldn't recall his name, but I knew he was one of the three big ego guys. I had hoped that by kicking one of them off, it would tame the rest. Was I going to lose this one, too?

"Can we talk?" he asked. His chest heaved up and down. I could tell he was trying not to let his temper get the best of him.

"Sure, um..." *Shit*, I couldn't remember his name.

"John. I am John." He sounded irritated by the fact that he had to tell me his name. I didn't blame him. I should have known his name.

"Right, John. I knew that," I lied, still riled up from the cursing match with Andrew minutes ago.

He rolled his eyes before he spoke again. "Right. That brings me to my point."

"What is your point, John?" I looked up at him, annoyed by his presence. I wanted to push him. He was a big guy; he could take it. Maybe I could punch him a bit too. I was tiny. He wouldn't even feel it through all those muscles.

"My point is that you just kicked off a senior." He ran his fingers through his thick, black hair. It was hard to tell the guys apart in the water. They all had similar physiques and wore matching swim caps. But, out of the water, John was exotic, perhaps of Latin descent.

"So what? He was a rude, snot-faced kid. I am his coach. He cannot disrespect me like that! He called me a bitch in front of the whole team." My voice escalated, unintentionally. I was losing it.

"Yeah. Well you are a bitch today," John leered down at me. Apparently, he was just as bothered by me as I was by him. I wished he wasn't so hot. It was a shame I was about to cut him from the team, too.

"Did you come in here to finish me off for Andrew?"

"No, I came here to explain to you that he is a real person - Andrew. Our *real coach* just died and the stand-in coach is giving him a hard time. Can you cut him some slack?"

"Calling me a bitch and a stand-in is not the way to get your friend back on the team. I'm no stand-in. I'm it – *The Coach.* Frankly, John, you are about to write your own walking papers."

"Frankly, *Coach,* I am about to quit." He raised his voice. I reached over and shut the door to the room. It was about to get ugly.

"Maybe you should quit, if you can't see that I was trying to help him."

"Help him? I saw you yell at him and belittle him. We all did."

"I saw his ego get in the way of his listening skills. I saw him refuse to take help from me. I tried to fix his stroke. I tried for days!"

"Days? That's what I'm trying to tell you, Coach. You tried for days and gave up. You started that fight this morning and you practically put the word 'bitch' in his mouth so that you could kick him off. It was an easy out for you."

"An easy out? You think that it's easy for me to take a kid's scholarship away?" I shrieked.

"I think you took the pussy route. You don't know anything about that guy, except for that you felt threatened by him!"

"Did you just call me a pussy?" I couldn't believe what he said.

"Yes." He got in my face. "Andrew has a six-month old baby. And you are a pussy." His smooth, bronze chest heaved in my face.

"You don't seem to understand, John!" I was angry with myself, as well as with him now. "It doesn't matter if Andrew has a baby." I pretended to be stone cold, but it was killing me. It actually did make a difference. It was easy to make an example of a boy that I had no ties to, but John had just made him real to me. I felt like a jerk, but I knew that if I took him back, the team would never show me any respect. At least if they were afraid of my tyranny, I would have an ounce of power over them.

"He's off the team."

"Pussy!" He said, lowering his chin to face my face. I felt his hot, angry breath on my lips. Goosebumps rose on my flesh.

I lowered my eyes and his pectorals jumped. I couldn't tell if he was hot with anger or caught up in something else.

The room suddenly felt sweltering. My body boiled with so many emotions that I longed to free myself of. I was scared, angry and troubled and I had brought it on myself. Now it was affecting everyone in my path.

I moved my mouth near his ear and whispered the word back to him, "Pussy."

His hand moved to my jaw. I thought he might be about to slap me, but his palm stopped and pressed to my flesh. Through his fingers, I felt John's impassioned energy. His rising testosterone emanated from his body.

John's tan skin glistened with perspiration, highlighting the cut of each muscle. I placed my own fingers above his raised hand. His bicep bulged from his electric arm; his fingers intertwined with mine. He remained still, all but the rising and lowering of his chiseled chest.

In an instant, every horrid thing that had happened that month flickered through my mind. I had to get rid of it. I needed to forget.

"You're right," I whispered, "I am a bitch." I turned to face his concentrated, brown eyes. I placed my lips on his, purging my troubles, and he didn't pull away.

"You'll give Andrew his place back on the team?" John asked me under my lips.

"No," I said and tasted his upper lip with the tip of my tongue. John allowed his lips to part and I tongued his lower lip. It was full and plump. His tongue touched mine and slid across the soft, pink skin inside my mouth. He began to kiss me feverishly and my troubles disappeared. Rage turned to fire. My hideous guilt-ridden emotions were replaced by lustful desire.

Our mouths began to quickly explore one another, seething, but seeking solace. I put my hand down his shorts and felt his arousal. He was big and hard. I ran my hand up and down his manhood. John breathed heavy on my shoulder, as it grew even larger.

He picked me up with his giant hands and put me on the table. In a sweeping motion, he pulled off my one piece and slid my ass to the edge of the surface. John bent over and kissed my breasts hard. His fingers drew down my side and across my hips, heading further south.

He touched my inner thigh lightly and I quivered in response. My knees fell apart. In a flash, he slid a sweaty finger into me. I could feel his anger inside my body. Juices ran down my inner thigh as he pushed it in and out.

I reached my fingers up to trace the lines of his sculpted upper body and kissed his hot, dewy flesh. My body wanted more of him, to be one.

He withdrew and I pressed myself to his shorts. He tore them off with a swoop and covered himself with a condom. (Where was that hiding?)

John's penis stood at attention and he touched its tip to the edge of my pussy. It drove me crazy. I spread my legs wider. My body pulsed and writhed upward toward his, dying to feel more of him. The wanton need to have his cock inside me was intense and animalistic.

I pressed myself even further forward and swallowed him inside me. I felt liberated. My head fell back as I let out a moan. I held on to the table to steady myself as he pressed himself in further. John thrust his pelvis forward and back. I squealed and bit into his chest the next time his upper body pressed forward toward mine. He moaned and slobbered on my neck.

I relaxed under his tongue and let him ravage me.

I wanted it to last forever, to have a big man in me and around me, reaching places that sent electric shocks through my soul; making all my issues disappear.

John bent over, wrapped his arms around my back and picked me up. I wrapped my legs around his hips and could feel him go in at a new angle in this position. He put his hands on my ass and moved me up and down. He drove in, each time, harder and harder. The insides of my body were stimulated beyond what I had ever thought possible.

Our bodies pushed and rubbed in frantic ecstasy. He placed me back on the desk. It lurched beneath the rhythm of our joined emotional tumble; each of us journeying inside the other. I stroked the mounds of muscle on his back. He wantonly kissed my lips as he gripped the metal edge of the desk. I felt his ass and appreciated how god-like it was; round, with a dent in just the right place on each cheek. I wanted to bite it, but I couldn't reach.

John's fingers made their way between our salty, wet flesh. He touched me with the intensity of a butterfly at first, then, he circled around my clit slowly. Excitement grew and so did my body. I became engorged under his touch. He pressed his fingertip to feel me and then I felt his own arousal grow. He began to move himself with vigor. I reached my own fingers through to feel John's delicate skin as I moved with him. I could feel his blood pulse. My own heartbeat quickened.

My jaw dropped and I squealed. My toes quivered as I came. He moaned in a soft low voice and orgasmed with me. At last – relief. John's body relaxed. He gently set me down on the desk and pulled out.

We each took a private moment to internalize what had just happened. I looked at him and laughed, nervously. We looked at each other and sighed as our adrenaline levels began to drop.

"Well," he began, "that wasn't exactly how I thought that was going to turn out."

"Me neither," I admitted.

"I thought I would either quit or get kicked off the swim team when I came in here," he said.

"So did I," I admitted, grinning from ear to ear.

I didn't feel ashamed or embarrassed. Nor, did I feel regret. I felt free; free to be happy. Sex with John had been feverish and hurried. It was the sexy fun I had been seeking and the attention I had craved. It felt awesome! When we connected sexually, I felt no pressure or worry. All I felt was him inside me, creating the most amazing sensations in my body. The world ceased to exist during our simple state of pleasure. And I wanted more.

I no longer cared if I was his coach or if I were married. I didn't care who he was or if he had a girlfriend. I just wanted more of him – no strings attached. Briefly, I wondered if John would go for a non-relationship like that.

We got dressed, aware that the lifeguards would want to get into their office soon. As hard as I tried, I could not wipe the silly smile off my face.

John looked pleased with himself. He knew that he had given me what I needed. There was a new effervescence in his eyes as he picked up his backpack and looked at me. I was sitting on the table that we had just done the nasty on.

"I'm sorry about Andrew and the situation I put him in, John. I know he is your friend. Look, I'll let him cool off for a week and then I'll put him back on the team okay?," I needed him to know that I wasn't completely heartless. I did feel bad about Andrew, but he put himself in the situation. I didn't force him to do anything. I simply doled out his consequences.

"Okay."

"But, don't tell anyone. I think I'll let them think Andrew's really gone for a bit."

He smiled before he continued in a gentle, voice, "Stop being such a bitch, okay?" John gave me a peck on the lips and turned toward the door.

"Sure. Today. I won't be a bitch *today*. You bought bitch credit for one day, John."

"That's it? What about Monday? Coach, you were unbearable at practice today. I can't take that again on Monday."

"Maybe... Who knows how long this smile will last?" I thought out loud. With any luck, he would come find me after practice Monday. I would just have to wait and see.

8

I was still smiling when I taught my speech class two hours later. As I led a discussion about nonverbal communication, I couldn't help but notice that Todd wasn't in class. That was a nonverbal signal to me. He had made a point of refusing to look at me during practice earlier and now he was boycotting class. I hoped he would at least show up. Not that I was worried, but he was missing some pretty important notes.

"Can anyone tell me what percent of communication is nonverbal?" I asked the class.

A few hands went up. I looked around the room and for the first time noticed my best friend, *Kamber*, sitting in the back. Her hand was held up high, of course.

What a know it all!

Bile rose into my mouth. At this vomit rate I was going to have to start carrying around a big green bottle of mouthwash wherever I went. There was no telling when she or Todd was going to show up and make me sick.

"Kamber?" I called on her out of curiosity.

"Ninety-three percent of all communication is nonverbal," she said in an overly perky manner, like she was expecting a doggy treat in return for her answer. If I had a treat, she would have gotten it – thrown straight at her head.

"That is correct," I responded. "And, what, may I ask, are you sitting in on this class for? As a journalism major, I would expect you to have taken this course your freshman year."

"I did," she replied, "I'm taking notes for my boyfriend."

"I see. And where exactly is your boyfriend?"

"He's sick," Kamber told the class and me. I let the conversation stop there. I was in too good of a mood to let the temper tantrums of a college boy ruin my day. If he wanted his girlfriend to take his notes, then I was going to let her. She was annoying, but at least Kamber didn't try to kiss me all the time.

I gave the class an assignment. They would have to give a three-minute presentation, instructing the class how to do something. The catch was that they could not talk. They had to rely solely on their nonverbal skills. "Have fun," I told them, "See you Tuesday."

I still basked in the afterglow of sex in the lifeguard office as I gathered my belongings from the podium before exiting class. Under my breath, I hummed a happy tune.

In the hallway, Kamber fell in step with me. I stopped humming when I realized that she planned to walk with me for more than a few paces.

"I don't think he's sick," she confided in me.

"Do you have a stick of gum?" I asked.

She gave me a look of disdain. I decided the easiest route would be to just play along and give in to her comment, which was obviously meant to lead me.

But, what was she leading up to? Did Todd do something? Did he say something?

"Who?" I finally asked her. My happy face began to droop in anticipation of what she might say.

Kamber's eyes widened and she moved her face uncomfortably close to my own. "Todd," she said. "He was in a rotten mood after practice. Then he pretended to get sick in the bathroom. I could tell that he had splashed water under his eyes to make it look like he was tearing up. So, I decided that anyone who would go to such length not to go to class should just stay home. So, I offered to go take notes for him."

"You offered?" I could not believe what a lap dog she was! When she spoke to me, I always felt as if she were trying to bully me. And yet when it came to her boyfriend, someone else wore the pants? That didn't add up. "Do you two live together?" I asked her.

"No. I just go over to his place a lot. He enjoys my company," she told me with a wink.

"I bet," I said. She didn't notice my acerbic tone.

"Yeah..." her voice softened, "but he's been real weird this past week. I guess the death of my uncle really affected him."

I had honestly forgotten that Sutton was Kamber's uncle. I felt bad for her loss, so I indulged her ego by asking her, "Have you found anything out yet? About Sutton?"

"Well," she whispered in the elevator, "I shouldn't be telling you, but I found something."

"You found something? What?"

"A note."

"A note? What did it say?"

"It said enough," she wasn't giving away details this time. Kamber was exasperating. When I wanted her to cork it, she rambled and when I was actually interested in what she was saying, she put a lid on it. She lost my pity vote.

"Well, where did you find this note?" I asked.

"At Sutton's house. I got Elizabeth to invite me over for dinner. After I encouraged her to drink three martinis, she passed out on the sofa. So..."

"So, you snooped around."

"Yup!"

She was so dang proud of herself.

"Big deal," I told her, hoping that an attack on her ego would get her to spill more details. "The note could have been from twenty years ago. How do you know it's relative to the death of your uncle?"

"Oh, I know alright."

"But, how?" The elevator opened to my floor. We left the dismal light of the small chamber and entered the sallow fluorescent light of the hallway constructed in the sixties.

I was shifting my bag on my shoulder when I felt my colleague's belly on my forearm. I looked up to see jolly ol' Professor Jack Jones. He was a cool cat who had taught in the building since the decade it has been built and I liked him. His beer belly represented his life. He was an older divorcee who "didn't give a rat's ass," as he would say, what other people thought. Although, he genuinely enjoyed the company of others, Jones enjoyed the company of liquor even more.

"Hey, Professor. Sorry about that." I smiled.

"Not a problem Templeton. I haven't been touched like that since a coed was earning a better grade in my communications law class this morning." He chuckled and looked entertained by the fact that Kamber shifted in her shoes at his lack of taste.

"Right then. I can see you are on your way out. I'll see you later." I never quite knew how to respond to comments like that. Was it out of line for me to think he was funny?

"Yes, you will. Let's meet up for drinks sometime soon. The gang gets together on Sunday nights. We drown our sorrows before starting the new week." He tipped his hat, adjusted his belt around his belly and walked away.

"Is that true?" Kamber asked me, more than a hint of concern in her voice. "Does he sleep with his students and give them better grades?"

"Geez! No! He is a nice old man and he was joking. Chill out."

"Okay. But he's creepy."

I ignored her comment about the Professor and continued on down the hall.

"So you went through Elizabeth's things, and..."

Kamber whispered under her breath, "Let's just say that I found it in her nightstand and that the police have officially opened my uncle's death up as a murder case."

"Whoa!" I was actually impressed. Kamber should be a detective, not a journalist. I wondered, not for the first time, if she had any suspicions about Todd and me?

I opened the door to my office and a small slip of blue, lined paper blew up from the door. A student must have slipped me a note. That wasn't unusual. I expected that it would be from a kid who needed to make-up a speech or ask for an extension on an assignment.

Kamber bent down to pick it up. I followed her into *my* office and threw *my* bag on a shelf behind *my* desk. She opened the folded notebook paper as if it was *her* note. She had some nerve!

Her eyes scanned its surface until her face turned white. "Shit," she exclaimed.

"What?" I asked. Kamber pressed the note to her stomach, as if that would protect me from its contents.

"What does it say, Kamber?" I tried to get the paper from her hands. I tugged on one corner and it began to dislodge from her grip beneath the pressure of my fingers.

"Don't tear it!" she yelled. The hallway was lined with office walls and doors made of nothing thicker than cardboard. Her voice echoed. She snapped the blue note away from my clutches.

"Then, let me see it," I said in a calm voice, hoping it would help settle her nerves.

"No. This is between me and the police," Kamber said and looked upward.

"It was under *my* door. The note was meant for me."

"No chance," she countered. Kamber was convinced that this note, under *my* door, was for her. Why?

"Jesus Fucking Christ, Kamber. Give me the fucking note!" In one swift move, I grabbed it out of her bony little fingers. She stared at me, her mouth agape. Was it the cursing or the snatching that surprised her? I didn't care. My own fingers shook as I smoothed it out and read the one word on the blue paper. I wasn't sure why I was nervous; accept that maybe Kamber's dramatics had moved me to a state of edginess.

It was written in all caps:

BITCH

That was it. That was all it said.

I was certain that the note was written to me, and not to Kamber. There was a long list of people who thought I was a bitch. It was a word I had gotten very used to hearing these days.

How self-centered was Kamber to believe that the note under my door was meant for her? I waded the paper up into a ball and tossed it into the trashcan to prove to her that the note was mine and, further, that it was of no consequence to me.

That was a mistake.

Kamber went into a fit. She shrieked and leaped over to the trash, dumping out its contents in search of the paper. Had she been a bit calmer, she would have realized that the blue paper was at the top of the pile; no fishing necessary. The girl was certifiable.

She was in tears on my floor, muttering as she fingered my trash. "You don't understand...you don't understand," over and over. She found the blue paper, flattened it, folded it and placed it securely into her bag.

I felt bad for the little nutcase, but I couldn't let her leave with *my* note. It was probably one of my swim team boys venting on paper. I pissed them off this week. Kicking Andrew off the team was a definite downer on my approval rating.

I doubt it was Andrew, though. He was the type to wait and speak his mind in person so he could have the satisfaction of seeing my facial reaction. Maybe it was Doug, the shy bookworm. He might be too shy to tell me his feelings of hurt and could likely choose a passive aggressive approach to voice his negative opinion of me. Yes, maybe it was from Doug.

I thought about John and my face burned red at the memory. He had called me a "Bitch" before he did me on the table. Maybe, it was a reminder of our hot angry sex. *Yeah, right*...I should be so lucky.

Deep down, I knew who it was. I didn't want to think of his name, but it refused to go away. There was no denying that the note had to be from Todd. He was angry with me for turning him down. The boy refused to look at me at practice and then sent his girlfriend to my class. Plus he was a bit of a text stalker. Perhaps, he had branched out to paper stalking. Maybe penmanship felt more personal to him.

The note was definitely meant for me.

"Give me the note, Kamber. It is not part of your investigation." I gestured quotation marks around the word, "investigation." She looked offended as I continued, "It is meant for me. Probably a student mad about a grade I gave them." I reasoned with her.

"No," she pouted like a child and swung her bag with the note inside behind her back. What did Todd see in her?

"Give me the note."

"Templeton, if you knew what I know. If you read what I read, then – then you would understand that this is clearly part of my uncle's case."

"Why do you think that?"

"Because, whoever wrote this note, also wrote the note I found in Elizabeth Sutton's nightstand. They must know that I turned the first note in to the police and now they are trying to scare me...or threaten me."

"How would they know that you would be in my office today?" I asked the little know-it-all.

"They are watching me," Kamber sounded so convinced that her truth was the only reality. I decided to give up. Some battles aren't worth fighting. I was tired of her face and her crazed super sleuth shenanigans. Hopefully, some of my colleagues heard our little spat today, just in case she ended up in the nuthouse or something.

"Oh, crap," I said, "Just take it."

Kamber practically ran out of my office. I could hear her calling Detective What's-his-name on her cell phone from the hallway. I shut my door, but I could still hear her through the thin walls.

I was so screwed! Certainly the note was from Todd. The detective would find this out and follow his trail back to me.

Suddenly, I wished that I was one of those teachers, like Professor Jones, who kept a flask in the bottom drawer of my desk. How could this not come back to me?

*****

"Professor Templeton?" The detective called through the front door of my house after he knocked twice. I began to move forward. My feet dragged as if there were one-hundred pound weights chained to my ankles.

When I finally reached the door, I pulled it open just a crack. I was so peeved about the mess I was in. How had I managed to screw up so badly? In all our years of marriage, this was the first time I had cheated.

I hoped to feel special through the boys' attention. Instead, I was feeling remorse – about one of them. I wished I could take an eraser and wipe out the kiss and the innuendo with Todd. He hadn't turned out to be whom I thought he was. That was my fault, though. I created an image of whom I wanted in my mind and I fit him into that box.

Now that John had stepped into my office and given me just what I needed, I feared that I might never get to taste his lips again as I eyed the detective staring at me from my doorstep.

I guess the shit had piled up. Two separate incidents, on two different days, with two very different people. Two plus two plus two equals a pile of carnage.

Now the icing on the crap cake - the BITCH note linked me, or someone I have been with, to a murder.

I eyed the brawny man who smelled as if he showered in a fish bowl.

"Hello, Detective," I finally spoke out loud, "Its *Mrs.* Templeton, not Professor." I flatly corrected him.

"May I come in?" he asked.

I was not born yesterday. There was no way I was going to let a grown man with a gun into my house while I was alone. "I'm afraid not," I told him, "It's a nice day, though. Shall we sit outside? I can bring out some cold lemonade." I was trying to make an effort to be hospitable. He did have a gun, after all.

He grunted, but accepted my offer, and guzzled down the lemonade as soon as I set it in his hand.

I didn't want to look like I had something to hide, so I came right out with it. "Are you here about the note we found in my office?"

"Yes. Kamber tells me that you didn't want to give it to her."

So, he thought I was protecting someone, I read between the lines.

The detective leaned back as to suggest that he were just here socially. No pressure - just friends talking. I didn't buy it.

"The note - It was in my office. Probably just an angry student or something. I thought it was no big deal. I threw it away." I told him, as I pushed my hair behind my shoulder. This was the last thing I needed, a detective looking into my phone records and following me around. John never called, but the text and phone records would show the endless times that Todd had called and texted me on my cell phone. I would feel humiliated if it got out.

I didn't want to get caught cheating. Although, the University never stated whether it was allowed or not, I was pretty sure I could lose my job for sleeping with a student. And, as much of a jerk I thought Craig was, I didn't want to hurt him or embarrass him with my actions. If I ever left him, it would be on my own terms, not because some detective found out that I was boffing the swim team.

Plus, I still held hope that things between Craig and I would get better someday. He didn't need to find out what I did to make it through the rough patch between us.

What a mess! My heart sank in my chest and I tasted metal on my tongue. Losing Craig was not an option. I had to be with him. He was a part of me. Mrs. Craig Templeton was who I was. I was a secondary character in The Craig Show, lately, but I would make it back to top billing soon. I had to.

"If it was no big deal, why didn't you just give it to the girl when she asked for it?" the detective wanted to know.

"I did… eventually. She brought it to you, right?"

"Yes, but she said that you put up much resistance," he continued.

I sized him up. He didn't look like he was going to give in. I had to give him something to go on; a reason for why I didn't let Kamber take the paper. Perhaps I could throw him off the scent of my adultery.

"Okay," I began, "You know what the note said..." I whispered the word, to imply that I wouldn't dare say such a word out loud, "bitch." I leaned forward and continued, "I recently took over coaching the men's swim team at UNLV. And the boys have been less than happy to have me there. Long story short, I asked a guy to leave the team and I think that it may have upset him."

"Who was it?" The Detective wanted to know.

"Well..." I pretended that it pained me to say his name. I took a dramatic inhale and finally said, "He has a baby, Detective." Hopefully, I sounded as if I were stalling for time to protect Andrew.

"His name, Mrs. Templeton," he pressed. The detective's face twitched, excited that he was squeezing information out of me.

"I'm sure he didn't mean anything by it. He was just venting on paper," I continued to sound protective of Andrew. (Andrew, who I didn't boink and to whom they would find no real connection to the note.)

The detective's eyes were wide. It was difficult for me not to smile.

"Andrew," I sighed, "Andrew Schaeffer."

"Thank you, Mrs. Templeton."

"Go easy on him, Detective, he's a good kid," I looked down.

"If he's a good kid, why'd you boot him from the team?"

Touche, I thought. "We had opposing opinions about the team." I said ambiguously. That was a good answer. This time I gazed to the right and crinkled my eyebrows. I was close to conversational victory; I could feel it!

"Well, I'll be honest with you Mrs. Templeton."

"Call me *Coach.*" I was just messing with him for fun by then. It had been incredibly easy to give him the name of someone who legitimately had beef with me and with whom I hadn't had relations with. *Candy from a baby!*

"*Coach*, the writing on the note you received matched the writing on the note we found at the Sutton place."

"Really?" I hadn't really believed that Kamber was onto anything with the second note until now.

"Yes. We had a handwriting expert take a look at it. The notes came from the same person."

"We just found it five hours ago. How could you get a handwriting expert to analyze it that quickly?"

"We work fast," he told me, "The expert just eyeballed it. We didn't run it through any of our software yet, but she's usually right."

"Phew," I sighed, "So, you could be wrong. It could just be similar writing."

"It could be," he began, "Or it could be that you pissed off a killer, Coach." I could tell that I had successfully pushed all of his buttons. He shoved his empty glass of lemonade in my hand and put on his sunglasses. He nodded and said, "Good day." The fish smell wavered on the porch as he marched to his car.

"Don't you want to leave me your card?" I called after him. The detective didn't even turn back to acknowledge me.

I had to be more careful, I reminded myself.

It was getting dark, so I decided to go back inside. Craig was on a trip to New York City. Puddles and I were alone together. I was so happy to have the little pee-demon at home to love.

I put some cat food in a bowl and stared at my phone. I checked my text messages to make sure that all of the texts from Todd had all been deleted. There was a new text there from *Guess Who* that I hadn't noticed before. It was sent at one o'clock and said:

WANNA MEET UP FOR DRINKS?

Was this guy for real? He hated me this morning and couldn't bear to be in the same room with me. He probably even wrote the BITCH note. But, now he wanted to have drinks? He was wackier than his girlfriend.

I decided not to text him back. Instead, I scrolled through my contacts and called Elizabeth Sutton. As the phone rang, I wasn't sure that I was doing the right thing. But Craig was out of town and I didn't feel like being home alone when the guy who killed Sutton was on the loose.

There was a click on the line and I heard, "Hello?"

"Hi, this is Susan. Is your Mom home?" I mentally prepared to invite myself over to the Sutton house as I spoke.

"No, She's out of town."

"Really? Oh, I didn't know that."

"Yeah. She went to New York City. Can I take a message or tell her you called?"

"No. Thank you. I'll call back when she returns." I felt my face get hot as I put the puzzle together. Susan was out of town. Craig was out of town. They were both in New York City. What were the chances that both my husband as his dead friend's wife were in the same city on the same nights coincidentally?

"When will she get back?" *Don't say Sunday*, I thought. I felt weak, like I might faint.

"Uh, Sunday...I think."

"K, thanks."

Was I jumping to conclusions? I have always heard about women's intuition and that women are supposed to trust said intuition. But, how can I tell the difference between an irrational fear and an actual hunch?

It all made sense. It would stand to reason that if Craig were sleeping with Elizabeth Sutton, then he would pay less attention to me and not want to sleep with me and he would kiss me like he was my brother. It would explain why he gets all excited every time he goes out of town to teach a seminar.

Then again, New York is a big city. It is possible for two people from the same town to visit NYC on the same weekend. I was jumping to conclusions. Oh, Hell! I didn't know what to believe.

The phone rang and I jumped as I scooped it up off the hook. It wasn't until I said, "Hello," that it occurred to me that maybe I should have screened the call.

"Susan?" he said.

"Yes," I replied.

"Did you get my text?" he asked.

"Todd?"

"Yes, Todd! Who else would it be?" He asked this as if my life revolved around *him*. How did I not see this coming?

"Well, let's see, Todd," *Don't provoke the killer*, I thought to myself as I spoke rapidly, "It could be my husband, a friend or *another* man." *Oops - Too much! He's gonna kill me!*

I couldn't help myself. I was eighty-five percent certain that he wrote the BITCH note. And here I was sass-talking an alleged killer.

"Where are you?"

"You know where I am, Todd. You called my house line."

"Can I come over?" He asked me in a puppy dog voice.

"No, sorry. My husband is home." I rapped my fingernails on the countertop repeatedly.

"Why isn't his car there?"

"How do you know his car isn't here?" I began to freak out a little.

"I didn't, but you just told me."

"Oh."

"Why did you lie to me?" Todd asked.

"I didn't lie. My husband is home. His car is in the shop," I explained to the possible psychopath.

"Well, can you get out for a bit?"

"No, Todd. I'm happy here, with my husband. I thought that I had made it clear that I don't want to see you outside of practice or class?" I had to give him the tough love. I couldn't let the stalker think he had any chance of being with me.

"No, you just said that you thought I should be with Kamber. You didn't say that you didn't want to see me. Can't we be friends?"

"No," I said bluntly.

"But, Susan, I thought we connected. I thought you liked me. That kiss was so hot!"

"Todd, I was confused and I made a mistake. I'm sorry that I put you in this position."

"But, you haven't put me in any position. Things are the same. I still love you. You still love me. I just know it."

"No, Todd. I do not love you. You do not love me. You love Kamber." The thought of him being with her creeped me out.

"I don't love Kamber. I love you," he repeated to himself.

"We are going in circles here. I'm gonna have to let you go."

"No! Wait!" He nearly shouted.

"What?"

"I broke up with Kamber," Todd confessed.

"No you didn't!" I really did not want that to be true. I wanted him to go on with his life and for me to go on with mine.

"I did. I really did."

"But she came to class and took notes for you this morning."

"What?" He sounded genuinely surprised at this.

"Yeah. She came to class and walked back with me to my office where we found..." my voice trailed off. *Oh no!*

"I broke up with her right after practice. You said I should be with her and I wanted to prove to you that I don't want her. I want you."

"But, why weren't you in class?"

"She took my keys and my car," Todd informed me, "She was upset. I figured she went somewhere to cry."

"Oh shit. Did you get your car back?"

"Yeah, she came back this afternoon. Gave me my keychain, left my car in the driveway and tried to fuck me."

"Did you?"

"No. I told her to leave and hid the keys from her."

"Really? Did she freak out? Smash your car with a bat or anything?"

"No. She cried. Then, she just kind of disappeared."

"Oh. Tough day for you."

"Yeah. You see? I don't want her. But, I need you, Susan."

"I don't think so, Todd."

"Why?"

"For starters, you text me too much."

"I will never text you again," he said so sincerely that I laughed out loud.

"You keep calling me at home."

"Your husband should feel jealous. Don't you like thinking that I could make him jealous?"

"No. I don't want him to know."

"I won't call anymore."

"You also told me that you loved me."

"I do."

"That's creepy."

"Why? It's how I feel."

"You should never say that to someone you've just barely started to be intimate with."

"I apologize. I take it back."

"It's too late." I was grinning now. He was so sweet and sincere.

"Please, Susan. I will only just think you are *okay* from now on."

"I don't know," I was beginning to break down. Honestly, it was really nice to have someone fawn over me the way Todd did. I felt flattered. My ego runneth over.

"How about you decide as we walk?" Todd asked me.

"I knew it. You're parked outside my house!"

"No, I'm not parked. But, I am standing outside. I walked over while you spoke to me."

"What about my husband?"

"He's not home."

"You're right, Stalker. I'll put some shoes on."

So, we went for a walk through my neighborhood. The sky over the two-story tract homes was black and lifeless. I felt the heat emanate from the sidewalk through the plastic sole of my sneakers. The warmth was like a massage for the sole of my feet. My body began to relax as we moved forward.

Todd and I walked side by side and discussed the upcoming meet and some things we could practice on Monday. He assured me that the guys didn't really think I was a bitch. I was not convinced.

"Andrew would disagree with you. You saw and heard him call me a Bitch."

"He's a dickhead," Todd discounted him.

"Yeah, well John had a few not nice words for me after practice today, too."

"You didn't kick him off too, did you?" Todd sounded fearful.

"No, but I gave him a piece of my mind!" I said. *A piece of me, is more like it*, I thought with a wicked smile.

"Don't worry about John."

"He called me a Bitch."

"He thinks all women are bitches."

"He does?" I asked, remembering the dirty words he had said to me. John was a sexy, sexy man. He was big and strong and took control. I wanted more of that!

"I don't really know," Todd confessed, "I don't really talk to John. I was just trying to make you feel better." He squeezed my hand. Todd was so cute! I loved how in control I was when I was with him. I felt like I got to call the shots while he got to worship me. It was a pretty smooth deal. *Maybe I shouldn't let him go just yet.*

Todd let go of my hand after he squeezed it. I touched his palm with my fingers and interlaced mine with his.

"We need to talk about Kamber," I told him. She was a serious problem for me, and for Todd, as well. I explained to him what went down this afternoon with the note and how the detective had already been to my house.

"What did you tell him about the note?" Todd asked.

"I told him that it most likely came from Andrew because I kicked him off the team."

"That was smart. So, you didn't tell him about me or us?"

"Hell no!" I dropped Todd's hand. He was taking the "us" thing too lightly. I stopped and put my hands on his shoulders. "Todd, you cannot tell anyone about us, okay? No one can know! I will be finished if anyone finds out! Finished! I will be shunned from the community. I will lose my job and I will lose my husband. Okay? You tell and I lose my life!"

"Well, I would make a new life with you," Todd said as if that would console me. He still didn't hear me.

"No, Todd! There is no life with you. I would be finished! I would put my tail between my legs and move back to Pennsylvania if anyone found out."

"No, you wouldn't. You could move in with me...find a new job. What's the big deal? You don't love your husband." Todd didn't understand my life. He never would. How could I expect him to?

"I enjoy the security and predictability of my marriage. Craig and I are having problems right now, but those problems will be distant memories someday."

"So, what am I?" Todd was so sweet. It hurt me to say it, but I had to be honest before he started texting me or something worse.

"You are a fun distraction for right now. I enjoy you. This thing between us is not permanent. In fact, I predict that you will tire of me before I tire of you." I tried to put a positive spin on it for him.

"I guess..." he muttered. We each looked forward at the long street ahead and resumed our walk.

He was so darn naive and handsome. I loved that about him. He ate out of the palm of my hand.

What was the harm of keeping him around for a while? He promised not to call or to e-mail anymore.

"But, Susan," he began, "I have to be honest with you."

"Yes, Todd?" I was expecting him to say something about how he still secretly loved me, although I had told him not to.

"Someone knows about us."

"What? Who?" I demanded to know. *Fuck! Fuck! Fuck!* I cursed myself for getting involved with Todd. He was seriously unstable and I had encouraged his behavior. In that moment, I felt dirty and creepy.

"Kamber."

"*Kamber*?" I roared as if he had said the name, Satan. "How? How the fuck does *Kamber* know?"

"You don't have to say her name like that."

"You mean *Kamber*? Fuck You!" I yelled at my puppy. He put his head down.

"I told her about us when I broke up with her. I didn't want to lie."

"Great!" I rolled my eyes, "Fuckin' great!" I said a few more curse words and stomped my feet a few times. My feet burned and my hands clenched.

"Susan," Todd grabbed my shoulder, "I think she already knew."

"What?" I paused my tantrum.

"I think she already knew. She had been acting weird all week. She mentioned that she had run into you at the mall. And the way she said your name, it was as if she was studying my reaction."

"I did see her at the mall. She was shopping for a birthday present for you. She made a point to mention that you were her boyfriend," I told him.

"My birthday isn't until December," Todd informed me.

"Oh, shit! How did she know about us?"

"She's a journalist...I don't know. I guess she has special powers."

"Oh my gosh, she wrote the note. She took your car, wrote the note and came to my class so that she could see my face when I read it!" I couldn't believe it! She had me duped! She had duped me more than once! I couldn't discriminate between what was true and what had been a lie. My mind was spinning in circles!

"What? I don't think..."

"Yes, Todd. She wrote the note. Who else?"

"What about Andrew?"

"Please!"

"John?"

"No!"

"Calm down, Susan. You'll be okay."

"Fuck you, Todd. I'm going home."

"I'll walk you." He was a gentleman even when I cursed at him! Yup, a puppy.

My voice softened, "No thanks. I want to walk alone. You go home. I'll see you Monday."

9

I debated about what to tell Craig upon his return. I had no idea whether or not Kamber would start a public smear campaign, but I had to be prepared for the worst. That meant that I must get to Craig with my story before Kamber told him her home-wrecking version.

I decided to seduce him first. I was feeling sexy and fearless since my surprise romp with John last Friday.

I bathed in rosy bathwater and covered my body with seductive smelling oil from Victoria's Secret. Over the oil, I rolled on white stockings with garters, a white corset that pushed my cleavage up to my chin and a little thong to match. To make my legs appear longer, I put on a pair of furry heels. There was no way he could say no to me tonight.

I stood posed at the top of the stairs, waiting for the sound of his car. He was late. I sat down and waited longer. Puddles came up to me and tried to rub on my leg, but I didn't want her to get her fur on me. I scratched her head and moved her away from my delicate stalking. "Mommy's going to get some from Daddy," I told her in my baby kitten voice.

I heard a car in the driveway. Goosebumps rose on my arms. It was Craig. I could hear his voice on the phone outside, but I couldn't make out the words. I stood up, posed myself just so, and waited for the door to open. I was ready for my grand entrance down the staircase.

His voice continued to bellow from the driveway. The front door did not open. *Who was he talking to?* My smile faded and my eyes dimmed. I walked down the stairs. So much for a grand entrance!

I put my ear to the front door, but I couldn't make out what he was saying. I moved to the front window. My nose pressed to the glass, so I could see him. He was pacing and talking; talking and pacing. *Who was he talking to?*

I turned my ear to the pane and heard a few words. "Yeah...me too...I know...fun...love...yeah....but I...I know...it will..." Craig didn't notice me in the window. He was engulfed in his conversation. All at once my mind raced through about seventy possible explanations to the scene before me.

Was it Elizabeth on the phone? Had he been cheating in New York City with the widow? When did it start up? Maybe it started at the funeral? Did they plan the trip? Or maybe they ran into each other there. Or maybe this had been going on for some time. Maybe Elizabeth lured us out here to get close to my husband. Then, when he had fallen for her, she "accidentally" killed her own husband with food poisoning and was free to be with Craig. All she had left to do was to break us up. That wasn't going to be difficult.

I slid away from the window and ran upstairs, suddenly feeling embarrassed. I put on a pair of jeans and a baby-t over my lingerie. As I walked down the stairs, Craig opened the door. Well, I got my entrance – in a pair of jeans. *Screw Craig! This was all his fault!*

"Hi Suzy. You look beautiful."

Yeah because I did my hair and make-up for you, asshole! I thought.

"Thanks," I told him in a monotone voice, "I need to go out for a bit," I told him.

"Okay," Craig said, "I'm tired anyway. I'll probably be asleep when you get home." He didn't even ask me where I was going. That hurt even more. Daggers pierced my heart in all directions.

"Bye," I muttered.

He was already not paying attention to me and on his way upstairs. *This was his fault!*

I got in my car and started driving. I didn't know where to go or who to go to. I just wanted to drown my sorrows in someone else's ear and if I couldn't find an ear, then into a glass of merlot. My lower lip trembled and I bit down. The daggers continued to tear at me and I fought to ignore the pain in my chest. *It won't be long*, I told myself. The UNLV pool wasn't open, but there was another place I could go.

I knew that the guys on the team hung out at a dive bar across from campus. Against my better judgment, I headed over to the team's watering hole.

The bar was dark, with blue lights inside. I could see the detergent marks on my jeans under the special blue lighting that college kids seemed to flock to. Pictures and knick-knacks were nailed all over the walls. I eyed the gaudy decorations and wandered through the dark. Eventually, I found my way to the bar. Something about the atmosphere told me that the place didn't serve wine, so I ordered a long island iced tea and began to guzzle it down. The daggers dulled a little.

"Whoa, you better watch it, bitch." I knew that voice. It belonged to the big, headstrong swimmer whom I had indulged in just days ago. *Or did he indulge in me?*

I turned around to face John. Relief washed through me and the pesky daggers were all but forgotten as I spoke to his chiseled face. "I thought I was a pussy," I countered.

He leaned to speak into my ear, "Whatever turns you on." He pulled his face back to where I could see it and smiled a mischievous smile.

I smiled, too, as naughty thoughts floated through my mind.

"Hey Templeton!" A big fat man on my other side cut off John's whisper. Startled, I jumped back and turned to see Professor Jones.

"Hey Professor. What are you doing here?" I asked, taking a mini-step away from the hot man who had been entertaining me.

"We always come here on Sundays," Jones said, gesturing toward a table of my colleagues.

"Of course you do," I grimaced. "Oh, Professor Jones, this is John. He's on the swim team that I coach. John, this is Professor Jack Jones."

John reached across me to shake the Professor's hand and brushed the side of his arm against my breast. "Nice to meet you, Sir," he said.

The Professor said something I couldn't hear back to John and then turned to me. "Why don't you come join us, Templeton?" he asked.

"Well," I began.

"What else are you gonna do? Hang out with your students? They don't want any of us oldies hanging around them." He gave my back a hearty pat and turned toward his group at a nearby booth.

"When you put it that way, how can I resist," I said sarcastically. "See you later, John." I wanted to linger there at the bar and exchange witty banter loaded with sexual innuendo with the hot, Latin swimmer, but it just wasn't in the cards. My colleagues were watching me. I didn't want to be tomorrow's gossip at work.

John caught my hand as I walked away. He pulled me close and whispered, "You're breasts look exquisite in that tight shirt."

"Thanks, you should see what's underneath," I tempted his ear.

"You are so sexy! I want you." It was enjoyable to hear that someone on this planet thought that I was sexy – *someone* wanted me. Butterflies fluttered in my chest as I walked away from John and over to the teacher table.

I turned my back to the booth of old fogies and gave John a wink before turning to join the ranks.

As I slid into the booth across from Jones and next to Dr. Caroline Crater, they raised their glasses. I gave Caroline's glass a clink before knocking my glass into the three glasses floating above the table.

"What are we drinking to?" I asked the table of Professors and Doctors.

"To freedom!" exclaimed Caroline, who slurred her words a bit. Her hair was brown and frizzy, fighting to free itself from the loose ponytail that had been doubled under behind her head. Her make-up was mostly gone. She usually looked so put together at school. It was nice to see that she could let lose.

"Alright!" I said, gulping the last bit of my drink before continuing, "Whose freedom?" I looked around the table.

"Mine," Caroline hollered, "Divorce number three! This time, the bastard is paying me! I'm so sick of paying my ex husbands to move out!"

"Here, here!" The crowd at the table pounded their fists on its wooden surface.

"Another round," said a guy I hadn't been introduced to.

I downed two more long island iced teas and shot the shit with my colleagues. I found out they were all divorced. I guess they had their own little club going on at the bar. I hoped they liked me, because I had a feeling that I could be joining the divorcee society in the near future.

I certainly liked them. They were a raunchy, lively bunch. No topic was off limits at this table. Everyone was drunk, free of judgment and a whole lot of fun. They yelled and spit when they talked. Their laughter sounded like howling. I was glad to have sat with them, rather than the young boys of the swim team. The bitter Professors' table was exactly what I needed.

"Can I call you a cab?" asked Professor Jones as the evening came to an end. I glanced over at John. He was playing pool with two guys from the team. It crossed my mind to stay. After all, I was still wearing my sexy lingerie under my plain tee and jeans. But, I decided against it. I did not want to be the drunken coach hanging out with the jocks hoping for a bit of action. It was too pathetic.

"A cab would be great. Thanks Jones."

"You've got it, Templeton. Do come out again soon."

"Certainly."

I caught John's eye across the room and waved goodbye. He waved back and returned to his game. It appeared that he wanted as little to do with me in public, as I wanted to do with him. It was the perfect secret relationship.

As I slumped forward in the back of the cab, my mind drifted to Todd. I should not have gone on that walk with him. It only encouraged his affections. *Fuck. Fuckin' Todd. Man I am drunk.*

I admit that it felt good to be wanted by him, but it was selfish on my part to entertain his efforts. Ultimately, I was hurting both him and me. Oh, and Kamber had been hurt, too. *Fuckin' Kamber.* I smiled and began to feel queasy. I didn't know if it was the Long Islands or the thought of Fuckin' Kamber that made me sick. I didn't care what the cause was. It was very possible that I might vomit.

I was too drunk to dwell on Kamber and her notes. But I couldn't stand it. My mind flashed hazy recollections of her recent behavior. Nothing made sense. Either she was some sort of conniving mastermind, a woman scorned or none of the above, and I had no idea about anything. Again, I was drunk to the point of numbness – nothing made sense.

"Can you pull over?" I barely got the words out.

The cabbie veered right just in time for me to lean out the door and hurl into the gutter.

"It's brown," I said, not very clearly.

The cabbie didn't answer. He waited for me to shut the door and drove me to my house at a lightning pace. I gave him all of the twenties in my wallet after he helped me to the front door.

I stumbled inside and rolled onto the couch. It was the first time I'd ever slept apart from Craig, while being in the same house as him. As I covered myself with the fuzzy blanket that I use when I nap, I thought about the metaphor of that moment. Would Craig notice that I slept downstairs? Would he demand to know why I had done so? Would he be worried about me? About us?

Before I knew it, I had stopped thinking and passed out.

Four hours later, my eyes flashed open. I was still a little drunk. It was probably better that way. Swim practice would be starting soon. I bolted up the stairs and ran some hot water over my body, gave my teeth a good brush, got dressed and left. Craig was still asleep. He didn't even bat an eyelash. I wondered if he knew what time I got home last night – probably not. The daggers reappeared and twisted in my chest. *Stupid Fucking Craig Show!*

*****

"Allright boys! Let's see what you've got," I instructed, still feeling a bit tipsy. "We'll run all the events you'll be swimming this Saturday at Cal. John, you get to organize it. You know the roster. Here is the order of events. Set it up." I blew my whistle and pulled a chair up to the side of the pool.

John looked at me funny. So I spoke again, "Lets do the 100 meter free first, followed by the fly and so on. You guys know how to do this. You know what you swim. If you are not swimming then you should be stretching on the side. When a heat is done, you step up for the next event." I blew my whistle, "Get to your marks!"

There was a bit of shuffling then. They were listening to me. It may have been inspired out of fear that I would kick them off the team if they didn't do what I said. I did not mind one bit that fear was their inspiration. I was just relieved that they were listening.

I blew the whistle again, "Go!" The guys out of the water stared at me. My buzz was starting to fade, only to be replaced by a budding headache.

"Don't just look at me," I told the guys on the deck, "Jump around and stretch."

"Bitch," John said loud enough for me to hear.

"Go fuck yourself, John," I said loud enough for him and the rest of the boys to hear, "This is my pool, bucko. I suggest you shape up."

"Yes, Coach," he replied, "Sorry, Coach."

"And you better swim your ass off today, or you will be hangin' out with Andrew."

"I was kidding about the 'bitch' thing, Coach." He began to walk toward me.

I blew my whistle, stopping him in his tracks. "Get back over there, John, and stretch out! I don't need you to talk your way out of it. You're in the next group." He made an abrupt about-face and walked to the edge of the pool. I blew my whistle to start the fly.

John did, indeed, swim his ass off. His ass, by the way, looked exceptional in his speedo. My hangover disappeared for a moment while I gave John's tan buttocks their due regard. That small slice of pleasure had to end quickly, lest someone were to see my drool.

I wiped my mouth and refocused on being the big ol' Bitch that the boys had grown accustomed to swimming for. The whistle made its way back to its home – my mouth. I barked more demands.

By the end of practice my head was pounding. All I could think about was Ibuprofen. I stopped the guys early. They were looking good. Times were down. A few had actually listened to my feedback and improved their stroke. That was something to celebrate. I planned to mark the small victory with some pills for my headache. *Yea!*

I darted to the women's locker room after practice. Practically falling onto the bench, I took a deep breath and began to massage the veins in temples that pulsed and bulged through my skin. I heard nothing but the pounding of the blood welling up in vessels of my forehead. I didn't want to talk to Todd about his love for me and I didn't want to have steamy, angry sex with John. All I wanted was to get the hammering in my head to cease its internal torture!

Beads of sweat gathered on my brow. I took another breath and found a spot to focus on in front of me. My fingers shook as I rifled through my purse. Relief washed through me when my fingers finally located the small plastic bottle of pills. *At last!*

I swallowed the pills from my bag, washing them down with water from the water fountain. Three big inhales and exhales later, I forced myself to get going.

I began my trek across campus, glad to have sunglasses to block out the glare from the morning sun, which felt intense to my corneas. My ultimate goal was to get to my office, but the smell of the coffee shop and the allure of caffeine drew me in. I entered the warmly colored shop, decorated with generic pictures of coffee beans and still art. It was a buzz with students. Some read on comfortable chairs, others sat with their laptops and a few were chatting across tables. All I heard was noise and the sound of the voice in my head, saying *get coffee now*.

I ordered an iced nonfat latte with no sweetener from a guy in a green apron who seemed way too happy to be serving the masses and waited for my drink to pop up on the counter.

As I stood there, pretending to read a text message on my phone, I noticed a familiar face out the corner of my eye. *Oh shit.* As luck would have it, Kamber was sitting alone with a textbook and a cup of tea ten feet away from where I stood waiting. I nonchalantly turned my back to her and hoped she wouldn't notice me. Who knew what she would do or say if she saw me there?

"Coach!" she called out from behind my back. It was a small coffee shop. I had no choice but to turn around and acknowledge her existence.

"Hey there, Kamber," I addressed her, sounding bored and uncaring.

"What did you order?" she asked, fingering her two braids which fell in front of her shoulders.

"An iced latte," I replied, realizing that even her braids annoyed me.

"Hmmm... I could never really get into the whole espresso, latte, mochachino thing. I've always been a tea gal, myself."

"Gee, that's nice," I told her, and before I could bite my tongue, I added, "Why are you speaking to me?"

"What do you mean?" Kamber asked. She smiled and twirled one of the two red braids that fell to the sides of her face.

There was a pregnant pause before I spoke. I didn't want to give up too much information. What if Todd were lying to me? Maybe Kamber didn't know about the kiss between him and me. So I said, "Todd told me that he broke up with you. He said that it happened *before* you came to my class last week."

"Yes… And what does that have to do with you?" she asked.

Was she messing with me? Or did she really not know what I was hinting at? One of the terrible twosome was a great actor!

My latte appeared on the counter. I picked it up and returned to her. "Well, I just think it's odd that Todd broke up with you and, yet, you came to my class to take notes for him. Why would a person do a favor for the one who just broke their heart."

"He did not break my heart. And we are not over. He just needs a little break. But, he'll come back. I mean, I am *trying* to get him back. I thought that he would appreciate the favor. Which he did, by the way. We totally got back together this past weekend." Kamber got all bouncy and leaned closer to me, "The make-up sex was the best ever!"

"What?" I nearly choked on my latte, "You got back together?" *Yuck.* They were both so foul! They deserved each other.

"Yes." She played with her stupid braid.

"When?"

"Friday night."

"What time?" My question might have sounded weird, but I just had to know if they got back together before or after I took that walk with him. One of the icky pair was a liar. And I still had absolutely no idea which crazy person it was taking me for a ride.

"I don't know. Anyway, why would my taking notes for my boyfriend, or ex-boyfriend, or whatever, in your class mean that I wouldn't want to speak to you?"

"He broke up with you *before* class. You were taking notes for your ex-boyfriend, *Kamber.*"

Her face looked blank as if she didn't follow my verbiage.

Okay, maybe she didn't know about the kiss. Was Todd a great big psycho liar?

I wanted to ask her about the BITCH note and find out whether or not she was the one who wrote it, but I had already said too much. If she didn't know about Todd and me, then I sure wasn't going to lead her to that conclusion. "Never mind," I told her. "I thought you were mad at me because I didn't want to give you the note is all. I can see that you are not mad. So, I'll be on my way."

"Where are you going?"

"To the Science building, to see my husband."

"Oh, I'll walk with you," Kamber offered.

Oh, HELL NO! And stop touching your braids! I wanted to say. I was so through with Kamber and Todd. They were going to drive me nuts if I let them.

"No, thanks. I want to walk alone today. Some other time, okay?"

"Okay," she said and took a gulp of her tea.

I exited so fast that I practically ran out of that coffee place. My feet didn't slow until it was safely out of sight.

*****

Craig had his reading glasses on. He appeared engulfed in a very thick book, when I peeked through his office door. I watched his eyes move from left to right. It was calming to be in his space; especially after experiencing the demented energy that belonged to Kamber just minutes ago. I knocked lightly on the doorframe.

"Hey," I said softly to the man whom I had once upon a time worshipped. I thought back to that time when I had pined for Craig in College. For the first half of our marriage I felt that I had hit the jackpot. I was so lucky to score a guy like him, I told myself. For years I had done everything I could to make sure that I was good enough. I always looked perfect and acted in a way that I thought I should act – for him. I did it for him. I lived my life for him.

Time passed. And after a while, though, the magic spell began to wear off. Craig was no longer the star of *our* show. He became the star of his own show and I started working on my own series.

I stared at the aged man before me. It seemed like eons now, since those days when I played a supporting role.

He looked up from his reading and pushed a bang from his forehead. Craig was not a bad looking guy. He still possessed every bit of star quality he'd had when I fell for him in college. It wasn't as if he'd shrunk in stature or lost his full head of sandy hair. He was still a few inches over six feet tall and his coif was as thick as it ever had been. The dimples in his cheeks imploded into his face every time he flashed his pearly whites, which I swore put off a sparkle when his upper lip rose to his gum line. I just couldn't see it anymore.

I knew others could see it, though. Women often commented to me about how juicy my hubby was. I liked the fact that they wanted him. He was a sort of trophy. But I also knew, that if he chose to do so, he could have any of them. That's why I went to his office this morning. I wanted to figure out whether he had made that choice or not.

"Hey," I repeated a bit louder.

"Hey is for horses," Craig smiled at me from his desk. He didn't get up.

"And sometimes cows," I added, returning the smile as I walked toward him.

He stood up, as I got closer. *Phew*, I sighed inside. It was a relief that he rose to meet me. I was beginning to feel like a fool until that saving moment.

Craig came around the desk. He gave me a hug and a peck on the cheek.

He began to break the embrace, but I pulled him in tighter. I inhaled his woody aftershave.

"We need to talk," I told him.

"Alright," he said and let out a huff, "When?"

"Now," I told him, letting go of our embrace. He sat back on his desktop. I leaned on the arm of a cushy chair.

"How'd you get such nice office furniture anyway?" I inquired in a pitiful little attempt to lighten the mood, "My furniture is from the dumpster and yours is from the Crate and Barrel catalogue." I fingered the fine leather piping around his soft green guest chair. For a moment I was jealous that he was obviously more of an asset to the University than I was. My own office was a hodgepodge of hand-me-down items from the seventies that I'd found in the basement of my building.

"I know people," was all he said in regards to my question. "Now, stop beating around the bush, Suzy. What did you come here to talk about?"

"Us," I told him.

"Us? I don't get it. What's wrong with us?" He touched his lips with two fingers.

"I think you know, Craig."

"No. I have no qualms. I thought we were perfect. I love this life I've made. I get to travel and I teach and I lecture and I golf...I golf a lot... Oh, and I get to see *you* when I come home."

"Do you know how many times you said, 'I' in that sentence?" I asked.

"No."

"Well, neither do I, but it was a lot. That is the problem. Everything is always about you."

"Yes, in my mind everything is about me," he admitted, "but everything I do is for us. I took this job because it came with a raise. That extra money is being invested so that we *both* can enjoy our retirement together."

His explanation actually made sense. I was starting to feel a bit ridiculous. Was it all in my mind? I didn't think so because I still felt like crap.

"Our retirement?" I asked.

"Yes. You know I work this hard for you Suzy."

"Really? For me? You work hard for me?"

He nodded.

"You work hard at going our of town and extending your trips so you can go golfing."

"You are being silly. I'm not going to turn down golf invites. That just doesn't make sense. And whether I'm here or lecturing at another University, I'm making money and putting in my time, so that we can both relax together someday."

"You want to relax together?"

"Yes. We'll retire in Florida in a over fifty golf course community. You can play bridge with the girls and I can, well, golf."

"Have you seen me hanging with any girls lately?"

"I can't force you to make friends, Suzy."

"No you can't. Not any more than I can force these Vegas hooker-look-a-likes to be my friend. Maybe if I got my boobs done, I'd fit in a little better around here."

"Maybe."

"Really?" My eyes widened. I felt self conscious at the thought that maybe I was a bit too athletic. Perhaps Craig wanted a woman with bigger curves.

He lifted his eyebrows.

"Do you think I need boobs, Craig?"

"I think you're just fine, Susan."

"Is that it?" I asked.

"Is that what?"

"You know."

"No, Susan, I don't know. What are you getting at?"

"You know," I repeated, "Is that the reason why we don't spend much time together?"

"We spend plenty of time together."

"You know what I mean, Craig. Alone...in the bedroom?"

He gave the blank stare again.

I was sick of the blank stare meant to make me feel like an idiot. Why was he making me spell it out? He knew damn well what was missing from our relationship didn't he?

"Sex, Craig. Sex. I don't feel any passion in our sex life, not that we have one anymore" I told him and returned his blank stare.

"I don't know what to tell you, Suzy. I try, but you put off my advances," Craig told me, his facial expression unwavering.

"That's bullshit. I tried to kiss you with tongue the other day and you pulled away."

"I've had a lot on my mind," Craig explained, "When men get stressed, they can't, uh, perform." The conversation got really awkward. Craig and I never spoke about sex. *Never!*

"Or, maybe..." Here I went, getting myself into a world of mess, but I said it anyway, "Maybe you are sleeping with someone else."

"How could you say that? You're crazy. I can't believe you would say that." Craig was still composed as he shot down my theories.

"It all adds up, Craig. You are always out of town. You don't want to touch me when you are here and..." I stopped my self.

"And what?" he spoke slowly and took my hand. *That calm bastard!*

"And you were in New York City at the same time as Elizabeth Sutton." There! I said it.

Immediately, I second-guessed myself. Was that an evil act on my part? If I was wrong, perhaps it was a horrible thing to say to him. If I was right, however...I didn't want to think about that. I wanted to take those words back. I didn't want to be right. I wanted my husband to lust after me. I wanted him to drool over me the way that Todd does – or did.

Craig let go of my hand. I had hit a nerve. *Oh geez! I* was the bastard.

He walked to the other side of the room and looked out the window. "Maybe we should never have moved here." He muttered, obviously disgusted by my words.

"I agree." I walked toward him, hesitantly. I was ashamed of myself.

"You are crazy," he said for a second time.

"Perhaps." I said.

"Perhaps yes," he told me, "You think I would cheat on you with my old coach's widow? That's just horrible, Susan."

"Well, the thought crossed my mind, Craig."

"That is sick."

"Yes. It is."

"I suppose you think I killed him too."

"No, Craig. Coach's death was accidental." That thought had actually never crossed my mind. I would never have suspected him of harming another person. Cheating – yes; Killing – no.

"Was it?" Craig turned around to face me. His face was a rare shade of reddish purple.

As, I looked upon my husband; I could feel the electricity flowing through his veins. It unnerved me.

I gulped down, fearing that he might actually hurt me. For a brief moment, I actually did suspect him of having the ability to kill another human. My heart stopped. I needed to take a breath, but I hesitated; I didn't dare move.

Craig stared at me for an extra second before relaxing his eyes of fire. He crossed the room and regained control over himself. I could almost see the thoughts churning in his mind. It was a full minute before he finally shared his thoughts out loud.

"Elizabeth called me, you know?" Craig began, "She said that you called her house while I was out of town last weekend, but you wouldn't leave a message with her kid."

"How'd she know it was me?" I asked him now that he appeared calm.

"The kid wrote our number down from Caller ID. Elizabeth thought that it was nice of us to check up on her. She invited us over."

"What did you say?" *Maybe I could look through her stuff.*

"Susan," he said. "You are missing the point!"

"Craig! What is the point?" I mimicked his tone. A small part of me wanted to make him really mad again; to see the less than perfect, more than piping mad version of himself.

"You called her to find out if she was sleeping with me!" Craig accused me, though his eyes didn't flare up this time.

"No, I didn't, actually," I really wanted to hit him on the arm with that fat book he had been reading.

"Why *did* you call her?" he demanded.

"I was putting together some clues, trying to solve a puzzle. I was hoping that she would invite me over, so I could get a look at her house."

"You are crazy! Clues? What are you? A detective? Susan? Do you expect me to believe you after you accused me of sleeping with her?"

"Yes, because I didn't think that you were doing, uh, *that*, until I found out that she was in New York City on the same weekend as you." I started to feel anxious. I needed Craig to listen to me. I was not crazy, nor was I coming to weird conclusions. The pieces fit together.

"Manhattan is a big city, Susan,"

"I know."

"I'm not cheating on you with Elizabeth."

"Okay."

"And I said, 'Yes,' to her dinner invitation."

"Okay... good," I said, even though I didn't feel satisfied with his explanation.

Craig kissed my cheek. "I have a lot of work to do before my next lecture."

"Okay," I watched him as he made his way back to the chair behind elaborate desk. "Craig?" I asked, taking one last stab.

"Yes, Susan?"

"Are you cheating on me with *anyone*?"

He looked up to make eye contact with me and answered, curtly "No, Susan."

"Okay," I replied, "I'll see you at home." I walked out of his office, feeling just as uneasy as I had before I'd started that argument.

10

It didn't add up. Was it my own guilt that was causing me to think that Craig was cheating? Were my suppositions unfounded or was my own naughty behavior in response to his wrongdoings? I needed to know where the blame should fall. Who was the bad guy?

A third party would probably tell me to stop fooling around with the boys on my team, to let my mind clear and then see where the pieces fall. Perhaps a non-emotional, non-crazy, third party observer would also follow said instructions and cease all relations with said boys.

For now, I had to focus on the next swim meet. Up until Coach Sutton's death, the men had had a really stellar season. ASD (After Sutton's Death), we were down a guy and our spirits weren't exactly upbeat. I had to rally the team.

We were swimming against San Diego State, a known competitor. I gave the guys the morning off, so they could get some extra sleep.

Our van took us to Mc Carran International Airport in the early evening. It was a medium-sized airport, as far as international airports go. It was adorned with crappy palm tree carpet, hopped-up slot machines and neon shops, Vegas style. Although, smoking was banned inside every other airport in the country, Mc Carran set aside lounges that looked like square fishbowls with smoky windows from improper ventilation. As a result, the hallways smelled a bit like the exhaust from dirty tar mouths.

Lucky for me, we didn't have far to walk to get to our terminal.

Our plane was going to depart in thirty minutes. I sat in the plastic seat and obsessed over the past scores for each of the guys. As a coach, I needed my team to do just as well or better than they had at prior meets.

"Want anything?" Todd asked me, leaning forward into my space.

"Like what?" I was trying not to lead him on, but I was thirsty. It had been difficult fending him off the past few days, but I think I was able to give him enough hints to get through that thick skull of his.

"I don't know. I'm going to the gift shop."

"Do they have water?"

"Yes, they have water, *Coach*." His voice got low and gnarly. I didn't like the way he said, 'Coach,' but I decided to accept his offer.

"Okay. I'll take a water. Thanks."

"I wouldn't drink that if I were you," said a familiar low voice from behind me. It was John. I had done a good job with him this week, too. Not once, did I try to hold his gaze or act flirty or needy... or horny, for that matter. John was a cool guy. He was no stalker. I think he liked having sex with me, but he was definitely *not* in love. He certainly didn't *need* me. I liked his independence and his lack of drawing conclusions about what had happened between us last week.

"Why shouldn't I drink Todd's water?" I asked him, looking over my shoulder at Todd's figure as he disappeared into the crowd.

"Well, he's our number one suspect," John entertained my attention.

"What?"

"We think that he poisoned Coach Sutton," John informed me in a casual tone. A few other guys nodded in agreement from their seats all around me. They didn't even look up from their books or text phones.

"Really?"

He nodded.

"Why didn't you tell me?" I shifted my body in the seat to better face him. His seat backed into mine, but his face was awfully close when I turned around. A jolt ran beneath my skin.

He shrugged in response to my question and gave no sign that he felt the heat of my body near his.

"Why haven't you called the police?" I felt so gross for having kissed the lying, stalker whom the entire team believed was capable of poisoning another human being. I fought back the sour feeling in my belly by pushing the memories out of my head.

"He's on our team. We aren't going to rat him out. Plus, what proof do we have?"

"You tell me. What proof *do* you have?" I asked John as I turned to look at the rest of the team nearby.

The guys around me shook their heads. John looked around at them too, "Nothing. But, he sure is a goofy guy."

"Goofy does not equal killer."

"No, but we think he was sleeping with the Coach's wife?"

"What?"

"Yeah. He dropped a note out of his bag once. Andrew picked it up and started razzing him in front of everybody. He started to read the note out loud. But, he stopped when he realized who it was meant for."

"Really?" John nodded and then looked up, "Hey, Todd," He said loudly to inform me of Todd's return. John spoke so loudly that I giggled. He gave me a soft punch on the shoulder and turned his back to me. I abruptly shifted around in my seat, facing my own back to him.

"Here ya go," said Todd as he handed me the bottled water.

"Thanks," I said as I discreetly looked over the bottle for signs of tampering.

"Aren't you going to take a sip?" he asked me.

"Later," I replied.

*****

I was seated in first class on the plane, while the guys sat in coach. I had never sat up front before, but once I got a taste of its luxury, I swore I would never go back to that toilet called, "coach," ever!

I had a glass of wine before the plane took off. In the First Class cabin the bottles of water were handed out freely. I had the flight attendant throw away the bottle that Todd gave me and replace it with the airline brand. It was probably fine, but if there was even a five percent chance that Todd was a poisonous killer, I wasn't going to risk it.

The in-flight movie was one with Matthew McConaughey and Kate Hudson. I was really getting into the zany plot line, when I smelled a familiar man nearby. I looked up to see John leaning on the empty seat next to me.

"I see that you're still alive. You must have thrown Todd's water away," he commented with a wicked smile.

"As a matter of fact I did. The flight attendant offered me something better," I raised my third glass of wine and said, "Cheers," with an equally devious smile. I handed him an extra bottle of water that I had been hoarding in the seat pocket in front of me. He clinked his bottle to my glass.

"What are we drinking to?" he asked as he took a sip and slid into the vacant seat beside mine.

"Victory," I said, in a slightly slurred voice.

He leaned close and whispered, "How about we drink to the mile high club instead?"

I did not even hesitate to answer, "I'll drink to that!" Before I could get the cup to my mouth, John snatched it and threw it back into his own throat, as though it were a tequila shooter. He plodded the plastic vessel on my tray and stood up.

"See you in the front," he said to me.

"We are in the front," I called after him.

He didn't look back. I watched him walk away and disappear into the lavatory. It was only five rows from where I was sitting.

It seemed to me that the lavatory was a conspicuous location for us to get busy. Our mutual attraction was supposed to be a secret. I briefly wondered if it was a trap.

No! It was John. He was a typical male in his early twenties. He didn't think about stuff that thoroughly. John was not out to get me or to out me.

He wanted what I wanted – Sex. My mouth salivated at the thought.

I waited for what felt like forever, anxiously shifting in my seat. (In actuality it was more like forty-five seconds.) Then, I stood and followed him to the first class restroom.

When I reached the door to the lavatory, there was an old lady standing there staring down the sign that said, "Occupied." *Oh crap*, I thought, as I pictured her knocking on the door only to find a big naked surprise on the inside.

"Are you waiting?" I asked her the obvious question in a loud voice. I hoped that John could hear me from the other side of the door.

"Yes," she said shortly.

"There's another restroom on the other side of the cabin," I told her.

"That's okay. I'm next in line here," she said, "You can have it."

"I, um… okay." I started to walk away, sad that I wouldn't get to play around with John. It took about five steps before I fully realized what I was about to give up – all because of a stubborn old woman. I paused a moment in thought and conjured up what I thought was a rather good plan.

"I'm gonna puke!" I turned toward her and exclaimed. Okay, it wasn't very original, but it was a means to an end. I was wine-drunk, after all.

She stepped to the side as I propelled myself forward. My body wedged past hers and I bent over in front of the door that still read, "Occupied."

I knocked on the door from my doubled over position. "Excuse me! I'm gonna vomit! Let me in! Please! I'm beggin' ya!" I was barely able to suppressed the giggle that itched at my throat as I waited for my partner in crime's response.

The door flew open, its occupant, still clothed, pulled me inside. "Oh, my," he bellowed, "Let me help you, Miss." John abruptly slid the door closed and locked us in.

Nothing about the First Class lavatory was first class. For some reason, I envisioned a marble counter top, fancy lotions and a masseuse. But, it was just as tiny and stupid as all the other airplane lavatories I'd been in. The only difference was the lemongrass-scented lotion and soap attached to the sink.

John looked at me began to laugh. At this, I fell apart. My body shook with delight. I fell forward toward him. My hair flopped into my face. At this, he embraced my shoulders as they fell to his large chest and he brushed my hair from my face with his fingertips.

I stopped laughing and looked at his dark eyes, full of joy. His teeth were exposed, shining white through his wide grin.

"What?" I asked. I had always pictured a sexual romp on a plane as sexy. This was not going down as I had fantasized it. So far, it bordered on ridiculous.

"Please!" he mocked me, "Let me in! I'm gonna yack all over the plane!"

"I didn't say 'yack,' I said 'vomit.' And Shut up," I teased him.

"Make me," he said, wrapping his arms around me tightly.

"That won't be difficult at all," I grinned. My arms pinned to my sides, I opened my palm and pressed it against his arousal.

I looked up to see John's face and his teeth sparkled at me.

I covered his mouth with mine. His tongue tasted of the sweet white wine he sipped from my glass moments ago. I pressed my pelvis to his and could feel his heartbeat in his pants. That was all I needed.

I moved my lips to his neck and tasted his flesh. It was salty and sweet, full of male pheromones. I kissed and licked him some more, wanting to eat him up just to have him inside me.

He bent his knees and reached down to pull my pants to my ankles. I slipped his down as well. His penis throbbed as he slid it between my thighs. It was hot and moist, creating the same sensation where it touched my delicate skin. My senses heightened. Goosebumps rose on my arms.

I groaned and gave his shoulder a bite. I ached to have him. "Put it in," I urged breathing hot and heavy into the spot I had just sunk my teeth into.

He reached his hands around to my ass cheeks and applied gentle pressure. His eyes danced as he pulled me in close to him. John whispered in my ear and told me to be patient.

He pushed his hips into mine and put it in just a little. I let out a small squeal. It wasn't enough. John was driving me crazy. I needed *him* – all of him - inside me and pronto!

"Come on!" I moaned.

"Beg me," he cooed.

"What?"

"You heard me," he grunted, grabbing my ass.

No way! I thought.

"Say please," he said.

I tried to reach my hand around him to swat his behind, but his back was pressed to the counter.

"Come on, Coach. Beg for it."

My fingers grabbed on to his shoulders then. There would be no begging. He would tease me no more! My legs wrapped behind his and before he knew it I lifted myself up on him and pressed my pelvis hard to his. His penis drove inside me, gliding in with ease. He was rock-hard and filled my warm insides with everything I had longed for.

It was John who moaned then. He was done for. No more teasing. He began to push himself in deeper. My thighs squeezed as he moved himself in and out with slippery simplicity.

My vision went hazy. I heard his panting and felt the musculature of his back as my fingertips clung to him, pushing my pelvis in synchronicity to his.

I quivered inside. John pushed deeper and my muscles shook uncontrollably around his hard flesh. My brain spun in my head as I came. My body clenched up and then relaxed in the moment that followed. I melted into the man who held my body.

"Coach," he moaned, burying his face in my chest. What a turn on! Hearing him moan the word Coach brought my body to attention. I bolted up and began to push back against John with fury.

"Oh, Coach," he muttered into the nape of my neck. It sounded so deliciously naughty.

A scream escaped my mouth and his hand covered my lips instantaneously. I screamed even louder into his palm. My pulse raced to match his own crazy beating heart.

There were moans, breaths, groans and sighs. I didn't know what sound came from which one of us anymore. Panting and pushing, we erupted together.

Johns shoulders fell forward and he caught himself on the wall behind me. "Coach," he whispered in my ear as his body recovered from the release.

My fingers slid from his shoulders and down the hard curvature of his pecs. I removed myself from around him.

John pulled out and he let out a sigh.

I bent down and pulled his pants up for him, before returning my own into their original upright and locked position.

"Thanks," he said, beaming of satisfaction.

"No, thank you," I corrected him. I felt like the lucky one in our pair. I had scored myself a young, hot Latin lover and at that moment, although I wasn't sure why, I felt like I deserved him.

John looked at me as if he was about to say something when the flight attendant came on the speaker announcing that we were approaching our arrival destination.

"Time to go, Sexy," I told him. Then I noticed that his hand was already on the door handle. I felt silly. He didn't need me to tell him that. John was independent. He didn't *need* me; he just wanted to have sex with me. That was why I liked him. He was the perfect fling – perfect!

I wandered back to my seat and finished my water. The woman in the seat across from mine gave me a funny look. I checked myself out in a small mirror from my purse and realized that my hair had gone wild. There was just enough time to pull it back in a hair tie and finish my water before the flight attendant came around and made us all put our seats back to their upright and locked positions.

Fifteen minutes later we were on the ground.

*****

"Okay, guys. You have your room assignments. I want lights out at nine p.m. Don't fuck around okay? Just go to sleep. No booze, no girls, no games. Just sleep." I said, as I laid out the law under the soft lighting of the modern hotel lobby.

"We know, Coach."

"Can it, John. I didn't ask for feedback from you. I know you guys have done this before. I'm just reminding you that the same rules apply. Come get your keys and have a good night. I'll meet you in the hotel restaurant for breakfast at seven."

There were a few groans, which I ignored. The guys shuffled their bags around and came and got their keys from me.

"Here ya go, Todd," I said as coolly as possible, trying to avoid the eye contact that he was so intently trying to make with me.

"What's your room number?" he asked me. I couldn't believe that the punk had the audacity to ask me that question out in the open like that. He was throwing a tantrum because I wouldn't give him the connection or the attention that he craved.

"What's it to you?" I asked in a pissed off tone. I hoped he noticed how utterly inappropriate (not to mention annoying) I thought his behavior was.

"What if I need something?"

"What could you possibly need between now and seven tomorrow morning, Todd?" I asked him in an overly sarcastic tone.

"I can think of something he might need," one of the guys volunteered from the group.

"Shut the fuck up," John told him, clearly bothered by the statement.

"In case of emergency, Coach. You should give me – all of us – your room number. In case of an emergency." He looked around at the other guys. They were in various states of being. Some were texting. A few were gathering belongings. And some of them were dialed in to Todd's and my conversation.

I glanced over at John, who was turning on his iPod and picking up his duffle bag. A few of the other guys continued to watch our exchange. I looked at their faces and said loud enough for the boys to hear, "I am in 611, if you need me in an *emergency*. We are all on the same floor. Have a good night."

I turned abruptly away from Todd and walked through the team. When I reached the elevator, I anxiously pressed the button, irked that Todd had gotten to me. Chad, a freshman on the team, stood next to me and smiled. "Don't worry, Coach," he said, "we'll be good little boys."

I smiled back. He was a good kid. I needed to get myself in check for his and the rest of the team's sake. They didn't need a bitch for a coach. I decided then and there to be a better person. I was not going to let Todd get to me. For that matter, I was not going to screw John again. I was going to be there for the guys at their meet tomorrow and when our trip was over I would go home to my husband and fix things there too.

The Freshman, Chad, and I stepped inside the elevator. John and a few others stuffed themselves into the car as well. The team and I were packed in like sardines and in the thirty seconds that it took to get from the lobby to our floor, John found a way to fondle my breast. I fought back a giggle and didn't dare look him in the eye. Behaving myself was going to be difficult tonight.

The boys and I stepped out of the elevator and dispersed in different directions to our rooms. I slid my keycard in the slot of my door and it lit green. As I slid the card of its slot, a familiar manly sex scent entered my nose. I could totally smell it on him, I mused.

"What do you know," John said, "we are next door neighbors." He gave me a mischievous smile. *Oh shit,* I thought.

"I swear, I did not plan this," I informed him, laughing to myself at the pathetic irony of the room situation. I did, however, make certain that Todd was in the farthest room from me. I put him in with Daniel. Daniel was a bit of a geek and could only see things in black and white. I knew that if I said lights out at nine p.m., Daniel would make sure that Todd would be locked down at nine sharp.

"Well, lucky me," John said.

"Oh no, you already got lucky earlier. You are going to sleep in two hours. So go take a shower and hit the pillow."

"What a bitch," he said with a chuckle. He liked my ornery attitude.

I smiled and shrugged.

He opened his own door and we parted ways.

I allowed my door to shut, set down my bag and took off my shoes. My first thought was to call room service and order a bottle of wine and a snack, but then I remembered that I had already had too much of wine on the plane and decided against it. I didn't want to have a headache in the morning. My goal was to be a better coach.

I washed my face and lay down on the bed. There was an old episode of Seinfeld on TV. I laughed at Kramer's shenanigans and my eyelids started to close. Elaine said something funny and my eyes reopened to watch her, but they quickly got heavy again. I thought about John as I began to drift asleep. The bathroom sex had been spontaneous, quick and awesome. He had a huge, hard penis and made me cum twice within minutes. John had covered my mouth with his big hand, so the people on the plane could not hear my scream. That only excited me more. It had been an awesome release. The thought of it brought me out of my almost-slumber.

In all the excitement, however, I noticed when he pulled out of me that he had failed to wear a condom. That was my fault I guess. I had been so caught up in the idea and thrill of joining the mile high club that I hadn't asked him to wear one. It was a very stupid mistake, which I hoped I wouldn't have to pay for later.

I weighed the possible outcomes and decided that genital warts would be the worst of all the consequences of unprotected sex. It was karma and it was catching up to me. I had to stop all the nonsense before I ended up a jobless divorcee with bumps all over her womanly parts.

I rolled over to my side and tried to let the characters from Seinfeld ease my worries. My eyes began to close again, when there was a knock at the door. I tried to ignore it, but the knock came again. It was undoubtedly one of the team, but it was a crapshoot as to which one knocked on the door. I was slowly pissing each of them off.

I looked through the keyhole and felt relief that it was John. At least he wasn't going to bitch at me. I could send him on his way quickly.

I opened the door. "What do you-"

John pulled me to him and absorbed my words with his lips. He picked me up off my feet and walked into my room. I clung to his torso like a slutty prom dress. As pleasant as it was being worn by a tall dark man, I needed my alone time.

"I don't think so," I warned him as my toes felt their way to the floor. I adjusted the wife beater I wore and took a calming breath. I was determined not to let his advances turn me on. Any other night I would have welcomed his advances, glad to finally have a bed to have sex on with him. But not this night. I craved some time to reflect upon the life I was leading.

John ignored me and closed the door to the hotel room.

"Seriously," I pushed him toward the exit, "I told you guys to get some sleep and I meant it."

"Sorry, but we don't accept the coach card at this establishment."

"John," I said in a low tone, as if I were scolding a puppy for peeing on the floor.

"Come on. Five minutes. Please," he wrapped his arms around my waist and looked down at me.

"Begging does not become you," I shook my head at him.

"Don't mock me, Coach. Just let me get some."

John was trying to use me to fulfill a need for power. It wasn't going to happen. I didn't want to piss him off and I knew that we had just done the dirty deed earlier, which was misleading to John. But, something clicked in my head an hour ago and I was finished with coeds. (At least I was finished for the night. Guilt had overtaken my lust for the time being.) Plus, his obvious display of an attempt to bully Coach Templeton was a turn-off for me.

I looked at him and put my hands over his, which were on my waist now. "John, I began, "you need to get some sleep tonight and so do I. We had our fun on the plane, but that was consensual. I am not consenting now."

The strong hold on my waist evaporated and I felt naked where his hands had just been. He took a step back. I raised an eyebrow, unable to decipher his facial expression.

"Why not?" His voice was somber.

"I realized something today," I began, looking into his dark brown eyes, "I realized that what I am doing is wrong. I am sure that this is all fun for you, what with banging your new female coach and all. But, the truth is that I am using you. And I don't like that."

"No, Coach. You're wrong. You aren't using me. And even if you are, I think I can live with that," John smiled at me. His fingers lightly stroked the skin on my waist.

"I'm not okay with that. And you are using me too. I am not okay with that either."

"You're not?"

"No, John."

"I think you're just being a bitch again, but... okay," He let go of my waist and backed away before turning to the door.

"Hey, John?" I asked.

"Yeah?"

"Don't go out and try to bang someone else tonight, okay?"

He laughed and turned to give me a wink.

"I won't." He placed his hand on the door and as he started to turn the knob there was a knock from the other side. It was a rapid and urgent rapping on the door.

"What the fuck?" He let go of the door and turned toward me. His face was red. "Who is that? Are you fucking someone else on the team too?" He stared in disbelief, "Who are you?"

"Relax, John. I am not sleeping with anyone else." I spoke slowly in a whisper, and then added, "Not even my husband." My eyes pleaded with his, begging for him to believe me. Since when did I care if John thought I was sleeping with anyone else?

John's face relaxed. He looked through the peephole. "It's Chad, the Freshman."

"I know who Chad is," I told him, "Can you hide or something?" I didn't need any rumors going around about John and me, especially since they'd be true.

The knocking occurred again. It was harder and louder. "Open up, Coach. It's me! It's Chad. I need you!" *Knock, Knock, Knock.* "Coach! Coach!"

"Hide!" I hissed at John, edging around him to get to the door.

"No." He crossed his arms and sat on the bed.

"Fine." I opened the door to see Chad huffing and puffing. He was frenzied. A few other guys poked their heads out into the hallway.

"Coach! You gotta come quick! Ya gotta see - it's it's it's," he stammered.

"What is it?" I stepped into the hallway and placed my hands on Chad's shoulders. "Chad. Take a breath. What's wrong?" He opened his mouth in an exaggerated motion and sucked in oxygen.

"It's Daniel. He's dead, I think."

"Let's go!" Chad and I ran down the hall. I felt the blood drain from my face. It was my worst nightmare. I was responsible for this team and one of the members was potentially dead - on my watch. *Oh shit! Oh shit! Oh shit!* was all that ran through my mind as I moved swiftly through the corridor of closed doors.

I tried not to panic as I arrived at his room. Todd was there, playing a video game on his Television calmly. *Seriously?* I thought as my face contorted into a questioning brow. I couldn't wrap my brain around what was happening.

"He's fine," Todd said, sounding bored. He didn't even bother to look up from his game, which was some sort of search and kill thing. The music had a supernatural quality.

Todd clicked away at his game controls and sounds of laser guns rang through the room.

"Can you turn that shit off?" I demanded in none too nice a tone as I made my way over to Daniel who lay on his bed. His skin was jaundiced. I touched his face. It felt clammy.

"Daniel?" I said his name loudly.

There was no answer. The creepy music went mute, but I could still hear Todd's fingers click-clacking away on the controller.

I bent over his face and heard no breath. His chest didn't move.

"Did you call 911?" I asked Chad.

"Yes. They should be here any minute. No thanks to Todd."

"He's fine," Todd said, still blind to the commotion behind him.

"No, he's not. Something's wrong!" Chad countered. He paced the room.

I did the only thing I could. I breathed into Daniel's mouth. His chest rose and fell. "Chad," I asked, "Come help me."

Chad walked over and began to press into Daniel's chest between my breaths.

Heavy steps pounded in the hallway. It was the ambulance. *At last!* I thought, *We have help!*

The paramedics worked quickly as Chad explained to them how he found him. "I came in to see if Daniel wanted to go downstairs to the bar. Sorry Coach." He looked over at me and I shook my head. It didn't really matter what the two boys were up to earlier. It mattered that he found Daniel and saved his life.

"Todd told me that he was already asleep. But, I really wanted to go drink so I tried to wake Daniel up. When he didn't respond I called 911 and went to get Coach," he explained.

"And you were here the whole time?" the medics asked Todd.

"Yes. I thought he was sleeping."

"Are you still playing your video game?" I asked him. I couldn't believe my eyes. Was he insane?

Todd finally looked up at me. His face went white. It took me a moment to realize that it was in response to the police officer who had stepped into the room behind me.

"Son, I am going to need to ask you a few questions," he said to Todd. "I'll catch you two over at the hospital," the Officer instructed Chad and I, gesturing for us to leave them alone.

The medics quickly got the gurney into the hallway and they were off to the hospital. Chad rode in the emergency vehicle. I followed them in the courtesy shuttle, which the front desk let me drive after a few tears and much whining.

John rode shot gun and all the boys who witnessed the commotion piled into the back seats. I ignored all the speculation in the vehicle as I drove. I already knew what the boys thought. *Todd did it. He poisoned Coach Sutton and now he was moving on to his teammates.*

It didn't make sense, though. Could Todd be capable of such things? Was he insane? What was his motive? Was it love? Did Todd write that letter to the Coach's wife, Elizabeth? Was he trying to get Coach out of the way?

But, that didn't explain why he would poison Daniel. Why would he do that? There had to be some other explanation for tonight's events.

The boys and I flew through the hallways like a hurricane of red and silver. We all had on UNLV warm-up suits and Runnin' Rebel t-shirts. It was what we packed for away games.

When we located the Emergency Room doctor, he had good news. Daniel was okay. He had stopped breathing for a minute, but the fact that we started CPR made him certain that Daniel was not going to have any brain damage. His heart had not stopped, but it had slowed down to a dangerous rate. They were able to get his heart rate up and had him on a ventilator to breathe. His blood pressure was almost normal again.

The Doctor continued talking, but I wasn't paying attention. I was so relieved that he was okay. John was next to me and I found his shoulder to let out a small tear on. He patted my back. A few other guys walked away to have some privacy of their own.

"When can we see him?" John asked the doctor.

"You can see him as soon as he is admitted. About an hour." *Whew.* I let out a sigh and broke free of John. I didn't want to blubber like a girl in front of my guys. I found a quiet corner to let loose a few tears before visiting the nurses' station.

I was dreading the phone call that I was going to have to make to his parents, but it turned out that the ER nurses had already taken care of it when he was admitted. I wasn't about to call them a second time. They were on their way. I could face them here at the hospital once they'd seen for themselves that their baby boy was okay. We would get through this night after all.

The guys went up to the room where Daniel laid in bed to see for themselves that he really was going to live.

I went to find the doctor. The hospital was a maze of white walls, locked doors and horrid lighting. I had to sneak back into the ER through the outside ambulance entrance when no one was looking. When I finally found the doctor, he was treating a kid who broke his arm fighting with his brother. I waited outside the makeshift room, separated from the bigger room by thin curtain. The boy's mother berated him for hurting himself and dragging her to the hospital at such a late hour. I listened to the lady yack at the child on and on and began to contemplate taking my own life when the doctor finally emerged from the curtain.

He sighed as he fled the scene of the yacker. Unfortunately for him, I jumped in his traffic pattern, forcing him to stop.

"Oh, excuse me, Coach," the doctor with a thick white hair said to me in a kind voice. I touched the sleeve of his white coat and made eye contact.

He gave me pause. The lines on his face deepened as he returned my look.

"Pardon me, Doctor, but may I ask you a question?"

"Sure. What is on your mind?" he spoke calmly, as though he didn't have ten emergencies waiting for him outside. His composure was commendable.

"I was wondering what happened to Daniel? Or, rather, *why* did this happen to him?"

"Well, I'm not really supposed to divulge details to non-family, but since you're his coach, I can tell you that we pumped his stomach and found Secobarbital."

"What's that?"

"It's a sleeping pill, Coach."

"A sleeping pill? Do you mean one sleeping pill or multiple pills? Did he swallow a whole bottle or just take one?"

"I'm not really supposed to answer that," he said.

"Come on, Doc. Please tell me. Did he take the pill himself or did someone slip it to him, like in his food or something?"

"I can't say."

"Please, Doc."

"I'm sorry, Coach. I have to go." He turned away.

The Doctor gave me just enough information to really get me worried and then he walked away.

I wanted to scream at him – to get him to turn around with a glare of terror in his eyes that mirrored the alarm that began to sound inside my head. *But he's a killer!* The acid words singed my tongue, but died there.

Sweat made its way to my forehead replacing the blood flow that generally ran through the thin veins in my face. I sucked in a hurricane of air in an attempt to catch my breath. My fingers, toes and ankles began to tremble. I began to walk forward, although the hallway was a blur.

That bastard, Todd, did this. I just knew it. His behavior tonight had been unbelievable.

My pace quickened as I felt the bitter soup rise from my gut. It found my mouth and I clenched my lips into a wall.

My fist's pounded the blue triangle that signified the ladies room. The door swung forward and I thrust my body to the nearest sink. The wall parted and the sea of vomit poured out, first the soup I had been holding in my mouth, which I felt a small wave of victory over. *Ha ha, vomit! I did not swallow you back down!*

But, the vomit wasn't giving up that easily. I felt more of the unwelcome sour juice rise up. I bent over the sink and let it lose.

That was it. My pulse slowed. I sighed and felt the color return to my face. My fingers washed the sink with a bit of water.

I wiped my mouth off with the back of my hand and went to find a vending machine for a water bottle.

The lights of the hallway were dimmer than I had remembered them from only five minutes earlier.

"Excuse me, Ma'am," a male's voice beckoned me from the other direction. I turned to find the cop from the hotel room.

"Hello, Officer," I greeted him, hoping that he wouldn't smell the vomit on my breath. I really needed some water or a toothbrush... Or vodka.

"Lansing. Officer Lansing is my name," he shook my hand and made great eye contact.

"Officer Lansing, I'm Susan Templeton. I'm sure you know this, but I'm their Coach."

"Yes, I know. I'm on my way up to talk to Chad – and Daniel, if he can speak. Would you walk with me, Mrs. Templeton?"

"Sure." The Officer was a big guy. He was over six feet tall and at least two hundred forty pounds. I was tired, but I wasn't about to piss him off by saying 'no' or telling him that I needed water.

We traveled up to the room and Officer Lansing questioned me about Todd. Obviously, he was Lansing's prime suspect, too. I tried not to reveal too much, only that he was an *odd* boy.

"Interesting," the Officer remarked and looked me up and down with a sneer. He made long eye contact with me again. This time it felt uncomfortable, as if he were trying to read my thoughts.

"What?"

"Interesting that you would call him 'odd' is all."

"Why is that interesting? Ask the team. They will tell you the same thing."

"Yes, but they aren't sleeping with him."

I almost vomited again at this. "I am not sleeping with him!" I urged him to believe me, "He is odd! He is odd! He is a creepy young man who did something unforgivable tonight. He ignored a passed out boy on his bed and refused to help him even after he stopped breathing! He is a son-of-a-bitch and I hope you keep him in jail tonight."

The Officer pulled out his notebook, licked his fingertip and flipped back a few pages. He cleared his voice dramatically and read out loud, "The Coach and I have a thing. We meet up in secret and make-out. I even went to her house once while her husband was out of town. I am in love with her." The cop closed the notebook as if he had just read a fact from the dictionary and then raped me with his eyes.

"No!" I shook my head. Todd was not going to take me down. I would deny this to the end. "He's lying, okay? The kid is more than just odd. He's crazy!"

Officer Lansing looked at me and shook his head. Then he stopped violating me with his stare. I could see that he didn't believe me and had pegged me for a liar.

"He's crazy," I repeated. We were outside Daniel's room now and I could see all the boys sitting with him through the window. They didn't notice us on the other side of the glass.

I whispered to the cop, "It never happened. Everything he said was a lie."

"Was he playing video games when you arrived at the scene?" he asked me.

"Yes." I opened the door then, wishing the Officer would lay off of me for a bit. We walked in to the room and I held Daniel's hand. He wouldn't be able to talk until the next day. Today, it was important for him to just continue breathing.

"I'm glad you're okay, Daniel. We all are." I looked around at the boys. They seemed to be at peace now that they saw for themselves that their teammate was all right.

"We are gonna go out and kick Cal's ass for you tomorrow!" one of the boys assured him.

Daniel lay there and tried to smile, but couldn't curve the corners of his mouth up due to the breathing device he bit down on. He looked much better now than he had when I breathed for him earlier. His face even had some color now.

Officer Lansing bullied his way through the room and kicked us all out. He wanted to talk to Chad and get a written statement from Daniel.

We took turns saying goodbye. It was time to get the team members back into their hotel rooms. They could use all the sleep they could get.

Tomorrow's swim meet was going to be tough, especially if Todd was in our company.

11

"Elizabeth," I said to our hostess as she answered the door.

"Susan!" she replied in a syrupy voice. We hugged and gave each other an obligatory kiss on the check. It may have been in my head, but I felt a weird vibe from her.

As I walked across the threshold to her home, I couldn't get one thought out of my head: *Is she or isn't she sleeping with my husband?*

Craig said hello to Elizabeth and he hugged her, as I had. My sick curiosity forced me to scrutinize their body language as they embraced. Were their bodies too close? Were they trying to hide something? I couldn't tell. My own body tensed as I realized that this evening was a huge mistake.

"Come on in, Dears," Elizabeth spoke in her new overly sweet tone, "Would you like a drink?"

I looked her up and down. Was she trying to cover something up between her and Craig with that smooth, sugary voice?

Yes – she *was* trying to hide something. It wasn't an affair, though. It was mourning. She still wasn't over her husband's death. Her eyes spoke louder than her syrup-coated words. Elizabeth looked forlorn and tired.

All at once I felt compassion and guilt. How had I even dared to entertain the notion that this poor, sad woman was fooling around with my husband?

Elizabeth was neither a killer, nor an adulteress. I was the only one at fault in this house.

I asked Elizabeth for a glass of water and Craig ordered a Jack and Coke. She ushered us into the living room and went into the kitchen to fix our drinks.

We sat on a couch and I squeezed Craig's hand. He was trembling. "What's wrong?" I asked him.

Craig took a breath.

"Craig?" I pressed, as I could feel his nerves through his skin.

He removed his fingers from my grip, looked around the room and replied, "The last time we were here was for Sutton's funeral."

Craig was the one who set up this dinner date. I guess he hadn't realized how freaked out he would be by the whole thing. I rubbed his arm to soothe his tension, "Yes. Let's try and be happy for Elizabeth's sake, though, okay?"

He winced at her name. "Yeah. Um, right. Sure, Suzy." He stood up and wandered to a decorative mirror, pretending to study the detail in its frame.

I didn't fail to notice Craig's out-of-character behavior, although I pretended not to read any more into his trembles. Since when did Craig's hands shake or his face wince? Nothing shook him up. Was he seeing Sutton's ghost or something?

"Hey, Craig!" said Elizabeth's child, bounding into the room out of nowhere.

"Hiya, Kiddo!" He high-fived the kid and added, "You remember Susan, don't you?"

"No." The child eyed me up and down.

"Taylor, this is Susan, my wife." He pushed the kid in my direction.

"Hi, Taylor," I spoke.

"Hi," Taylor said in a downer voice, refusing to look in my general direction. The child did an about face and exited the room. That was some welcome! The kid might as well have spat on me.

"That was weird. I don't usually have that effect on children." I commented to my husband.

"Yeah. I guess –" Craig paused his speech as Elizabeth re-entered with a tray of three drinks and a plastic smile.

She passed them out and we said a fake cheers, clinking our glasses together and sipping our drinks. Each of us fixed our face into an expression of what we thought appeared to express satisfaction. We spoke about the weather, sports and dinner recipes. Conversation was very awkward and dragged on for what felt like hours. Apparently, hanging out with recently widowed women was not a funfest at all.

After eons passed, we sat down to dinner. Elizabeth coaxed Taylor to the table and served up a table full of delectable foods. There was lamb, mushroom risotto, salad, bread with olive oil, roasted asparagus and rice pilaf.

Elizabeth was some chef! And Craig could not shut up about it. He would taste something slowly and then make little noises as he chewed. "Mmmmm...yummmm," he moaned with the food in his mouth.

Between each bite he would compliment her. "Oh, Elizabeth," he crooned, "I *love* this lamb!"

Then, he would eat a bit more and tell her how the asparagus made him weak in the knees. *Yuck!* What a suck-up. It was one thing to smile for the widow, but it was quite another to make a scene of lusting over the meal she'd prepared.

"Thanks, Craig." she said, robotically responding to his praises. She didn't even look up at him while he crooned. He was making the uncomfortable meal worse.

"Craig," I tried to say in a whisper, "I think you're embarrassing her." I kicked him under the table.

"What?" He mouthed, leering across the shiny dining table's surface. "Can't I compliment the chef on such a mouth-watering meal? I'm just being polite." He kicked me back, hard! Apparently, it was me who was embarrassing *him*.

"Ouch," I squealed, unable to sensor my response.

"What's wrong?" Craig looked at me with concern, as if he hadn't just made a welt on my shin.

I didn't answer him. I had already started a scene and I didn't want it to progress any further. Now, I was the one who felt embarrassed. A tear stung my eye.

"You be nice to Craig!" Taylor blurted out.

"Taylor!" Elizabeth hissed at the child across the table.

"It's okay," I assured her. "May I please use your restroom?"

"Certainly. It's right down the hall."

"Thanks." I excused myself and practically ran to the bathroom. I peed, washed my hands and ran some water over my face. As I dabbed my face with a towel, I thought about Craig's behavior. Was he trying to send me a signal? Did he wish that I cooked for him? Was he trying to point out that he could *love* that kind of a lady – a cook?

My gut told me otherwise. Besides, there was only one room in the house where I excelled and it wasn't the kitchen. I doubted it ever would be.

I tiptoed through the hallway and into the office. I figured that the ever annoying and always crazy, *Kamber*, had already scoped out the bedroom, so why waste what precious minutes I had alone snooping around in there?

The tiffany lamp on the table clicked on and offered up a soft glow against the dark space, barely enough to read by. I didn't see a wall switch or a light overhead and wondered how often Coach and Elizabeth actually utilized the his and hers desk space. It felt like a detective's office from the 1920's. And I was beginning to feel like a sleuth, myself.

I did not know exactly what I was looking for. Who-done-it type evidence maybe. *If only I had a cool cap and a magnifying glass,* I thought.

I lifted the papers on the top of the desk and browsed a bit. There were mostly bills and a few sympathy cards. I opened the drawers and rifled through pens, paperweights, post-its and paperclips. Nothing.

I stood up and walked around the room, touching books and tchokes. I picked up a picture of Taylor as a baby. There was a picture of Elizabeth at the beach. I noticed that there were no pictures of Coach Sutton in the office anywhere.

I could hear their muffled voices in the dining room. I wanted to know what they spoke about, but I wasn't yet satisfied with my search.

My eyes explored the room. I pulled open a drawer from the built-in bookcase and sifted through more stuff. There was a stack of pictures. I recognized them from Pennsylvania. The photos must have belonged to Coach Sutton because Elizabeth and he had met in Las Vegas. I felt a wave of nostalgia as I saw photos of old friends and old places. They held such fond memories for me! There was a picture of Craig with Coach Sutton from when he was a swimmer on his team at Penn. There was a group photo of the whole team. Dozens of photos showed Sutton's two grown children playing sports when they were young. There was a picture from a vacation our little friend group had taken to New York City when Craig and I had first started teaching.

I picked up the next set of photos and riffled through. There were a few more pictures of Craig at various places. I felt the hair on my arms raise up.

Then I found it - the mother load. My fingers trembled as I clasped the evidence that I had been looking for. My eyes bulged in disbelief. It was a picture of Craig and Elizabeth together! Their arms were wrapped around each other's shoulders. They were smiling like a couple on vacation.

Yes, logically, it was just a picture of Craig with his arm around our friend's wife. But, women's intuition told me otherwise. The fact was that he wasn't sleeping with me. But, he was in another room speaking in hushed tones a woman who has multiple pictures of him in a drawer.

Son of a Bitch!

I was hoping that Todd's story wasn't true, but there it was. The proof I had sought was right in front of my eyes. These weren't Coach's pictures. They were photos that Elizabeth was hoarding for herself.

I took the picture of them together and put it in my pocket. Anger kept me from crying. My fingers continued to shake until I forced them closed into a fist. The lines in my face set into a stoic expression. I was seething to the point of stillness. I held it together, much in the way Craig did so often.

Slowly, I crept back toward the dining room. I tried desperately to listen in on their conversation.

"It will get better," Craig told Elizabeth.

I couldn't hear her reply, so I inched closer.

"Boo!" screamed Taylor, jumping around the corner. "I got you!" the kid said and ran past me. That was my cue to enter.

"I'm back," I announced to the slime ball bastard and his slutty woman friend. I tried to look calm as fury built up inside me. A zillion thoughts went through my head all at once. My eyes squinted as I tried to regain focus. The room in front of me appeared soft then crisp, soft then crisp. I blinked a few times and it became clear again.

The couch felt cold as I perched myself in a cross-legged pose that I hoped looked casual. Craig said nothing more about Elizabeth's fantastic cooking.

Elizabeth asked me about the swim team. I didn't want to tell her how horrible it had been trying to fill the shoes of the dead man, whom she had so obviously murdered. I didn't want to tell her about the near-death episode a couple nights ago or about how the team had swum their worst times ever at the meet the following morning. I didn't want her to know that I had taken a group of young, hopeful athletes and crushed their dreams, kicked them out, gotten them hurt, driven them crazy and stomped on their hearts.

"They are coming out of a rough patch," I told her, "They'll be back on their A-game again soon." *Have I mentioned that you're a Whore?*

"Huh," she replied and looked to Craig blankly. With that, he told her that we had an early morning tomorrow and had to go. She rushed us out like we were trying to beat a flood.

Elizabeth said goodbye with her sad, adulteress, man-eater eyes and we left.

I held my breath the entire way home. I had to wait for the right moment to confront him. It had gone so horribly the last time I'd asked him about things with Elizabeth.

Craig sat in silence, as well. I wondered what he was thinking. Logic told me to keep my mouth shut, but curiosity overruled. So, I asked, "What are you thinking about?"

"Just stuff."

"What kind of stuff?"

"Life stuff. You know, how things end up the way they do. The irony of it all."

"What kind of irony? Death irony?"

"Sure, death. Circumstances..." his voice trailed off.

Was he thinking about *her*? This was driving me nuts! I realized the irony of my own anger toward Craig's behavior. It didn't change how I felt.

Craig slept with Elizabeth (still was from what I gathered.) And I slept with a college co-ed. That didn't make us even. I didn't have feelings for John.

If Craig were with Coach Sutton's wife, it could only be because he loved her. He could have his pick of any woman to cheat with. Love was the only thing that would make hurting his college coach and his adoring wife worthwhile.

"Do you still love me?" The words escaped my lips before I could force my defiant lips closed. Instantly, my heart began to beat fast. My ears burned. There was a ringing in my head.

I realized that I didn't want to know the answer to that question. I wanted to swallow my words and take it back. I wished that I could pretend that none of this was happening. I wanted to let it blow over and patch things up with my husband later.

Craig didn't answer me. It was a horrible, heart-achy moment. Then it got worse.

"I don't know," he said.

A lump grew large in my throat.

I   couldn't   breathe.

Tears welled up in my eyes.

It was the worst thing he had ever said to me and I had brought it upon myself. My stomach knotted up in an unbearable pain.

My jaw dropped and I gaped at him. I didn't believe him. He didn't say what I thought I had just heard. I was imagining this. I looked down at my shoes and wrapped my arms around my waist in an effort to comfort my belly.

"You don't know?" I dared to ask as the first tear of pain fell down my face.

He didn't look at me. I wanted him to do it – to see the pounding ache of emotional writhing he was causing me. "I don't know," he repeated.

My throat swelled up and my chin quivered. I started to cry out loud, full throttle. The idea that the man I had married didn't love me was traumatizing. The sudden wash of emotion caused horrid physical pain through my body. I doubled over and moaned into my arms, rocking forward and back.

"Oh shit," he said.

That was the most emotion I had seen out of him since Coach died, I thought.

"Don't cry," the unemotional jerk said to me. I turned my tear-strewn face to see him. Craig still didn't even look over to my side of the vehicle!

In *The Susan Show*, the husband dramatically pulls the car to the side of the road, turns it off and has a deep heart to heart conversation. *The Craig Show* wasn't stopping.

"Don't cry," he repeated.

"I can't help it," I roared. "You don't love me." The sobs continued.

"I didn't say that."

"You didn't say that you *did* love me."

"But, I didn't say that I didn't. Jesus, Suzy! You are so overdramatic!"

"Only when you don't love me!"

"I do. Okay? I do love you," he quickly admitted. It sounded like he was distressed to say the word, "love."

"Then why did you say that you didn't know?" I asked as my tears continued to pour.

"Because, things have been really weird lately."

"Ya think?" I asked.

"Yeah. I don't know. Ever since Sutton died, things have been weird."

My tears subsided and I tried to catch my breath as I processed Craig's words. "Things have been weird for me ever since we moved out here." I told him.

He waited to respond. Perhaps he was weighing his words. "You were just as excited as I was about the opportunity here, Susan."

"I was excited for *you*," I stressed. "I am sacrificing for you. I left my friends and family back East." My sobs got loud again.

"So did I."

"Yeah, but your sacrifice came with a cool new job. Mine comes with nothing. There are no friends out here for me. Nothing."

"You're still being overdramatic."

"No, I'm not. You get to go off to cool exciting places and do your seminars, while I get to stay at home with Puddles and drink wine alone."

"Oh my God. You are really starting to piss me off! It isn't up to me to make friends for you, Suzy. Start talking to people if you're so lonely. Besides, I got you that position coaching the swim team. I did that selflessly for you, so that you would have something meaningful out here. You don't even know how difficult it was for me to get that for you! And then you made me feel like *you* were doing *me* a favor by accepting the position!"

"You pulled strings?" I couldn't believe it. Craig had noticed that I was unhappy. I had no idea that he had tried to pull me out of my funk. A wave of huge shame washed over me. The tears continued, but the sobs had been replaced by deep inhales.

"Yes, Susan. I pulled strings." No sarcasm – he was really angry now. "I helped get you your teaching job at the University. That didn't make you happy. So then I sweet-talked the Athletic Director into giving you Coach's job when he passed away. And it seems you are managing to fuck that up too. You are leaving quite a trail of destructive behavior in your path. I regret that I am tangled up in it. I should have just backed off and let you create your own destiny because it seems you are determined to be unhappy."

"I am not determined to be unhappy," I defended myself, but I knew that he had a point.

"Yes, you are." He pulled into the garage, turned off the car and slammed the door upon his exit.

Okay, so this was all my fault. It still didn't explain why the intimacy in our relationship had disappeared. Why I'd cheated with a twenty-one-year-old from the swim team.

I could think of only one explanation. But, now was not the time. Craig was angry and I would never get the truth about Elizabeth from him tonight. I might never get the truth from him ever.

Before I approached Craig again about the realities of our situation, I would have to get more proof. All I had was a photo and my instincts to go on for now.

For tonight, having him say that he loved me would have to suffice. Anything was better than not being loved.

*****

"I didn't kill anyone!" I heard Todd through the door of the Detective's barren office.

I sat outside, waiting my turn to answer more questions from the cold man who had interrogated me at my house days ago. The two men's voices raised and then lowered at about two minute intervals.

My knee nervously bounced up and down as my mind reeled over all the recent shenanigans in which I'd become entangled. My heartbeat quickened. Was Detective on to me? Did he know about Todd or John or both? Did he think I had some privy information that he was going to weasel out of me? Did he think I was an accessory to something?

I could hear the defensive tone in Todd's voice. It sickened me to think that I had kissed a possible killer. But, I couldn't actually believe that Todd would poison two people. He seemed like a slightly irregular boy, but not a killer. Something didn't add up.

I continued waiting. Every few minutes I checked my watch, wondering when I could get back to school for office hours. After three watch checks, Todd thrust the door open and spoke loudly, "You can't hold me! All you have are two notes. You can't prove that I killed anyone! I'm out of here."

Todd began to storm heavily through the hall when he noticed me sitting there. He stopped. His chest heaved up and down. He stared into my eyes. "Tell him, Susan. Tell him I didn't do it."

"Todd," I began, "You know, we haven't known each other very long."

"Shit!" he yelled at me. "You think I did it too!"

He threw his hands in the air, defeated, and turned to leave. His hands balled into tight fists as he hastened away.

Just when I thought things would quiet down, I heard the most annoying sound in the world. "Honey!" screeched Kamber, running to Todd down the hallway, "Calm down. I'm here. I'm here. It's okay. I'll help you. We'll get through this."

Why couldn't she have found him in the parking lot?

She put her arm around him. He dropped his head and Kamber petted his hair with her fingers. She walked her boyfriend out of the precinct. I almost felt bad for him. Wait – no I didn't.

The Detective ushered me in. I read the placard on his desk, "Frank Buster."

"Thanks for meeting with me, Susan," the Detective sat across from me.

"Sure, Frank." I mocked his casual usage of my first name by calling him by his own first name.

"Your student, Todd, called you 'Susan,' so I thought that's what you preferred people call you. Or do only your students get to speak to you with such informality?" He picked up a pencil and chewed on the end of it.

"No. Not at all." As I spoke to him, I felt like a teenager called in to the Principal's office during lunch time. I wanted him to know that I felt put out by being beckoned into the station.

"Then, I guess what Todd told me is true, *Mrs. Templeton.*" He took the pencil out of his mouth and glared at me.

Oh Geez! "What did he tell you?" I tried not to sound humiliated and anxious. Though, that's exactly what I felt. My face burned from ear to ear. I felt my forehead sweat. Detective Frank was probably trained in picking up on these subconscious signals my body was sending him without my permission.

As I suspected, he saw right through me. "Todd said you two were intimate."

"Intimate? No. We were not intimate. I am married, Frank."

"And?"

"And I don't want to hurt my husband."

"But you did hurt him. He just doesn't know it. Don't bullshit me. Your face is purple and you are sweatin' bullets. It's not my first day on the job. Just tell me the truth so I can close this case."

"Which case?"

"Coach Sutton. How many cases are you involved in, *Susan?*"

"Not me! Todd. Todd is involved." I told the Detective about the trip to California and Daniel's near death experience.

"Huh. That certainly puts things in perspective. I'll call the department over in Berkley and get the details of the Daniel incident."

"So you think Todd did it?" I asked him.

"I never presume to think anything. I let the evidence tell me." He puffed his chest out like a proud bird. *What a Dick!* I thought.

"And what does the evidence tell you? Did Todd write those letters?"

"Yes."

"He wrote the bitch note to me!" I still couldn't believe it. I had actually hoped that it was Kamber's work.

"Yes."

"And he wrote to Elizabeth Sutton."

"Yes."

"What did the note to Elizabeth say?"

"I can't tell you that."

"I will tell you about him and me if you tell me what was in that note found in Sutton's house?"

"Let's just say it was a love letter. You weren't the first married woman he had a fling with, Susan." He chewed on his pencil again and studied my face. "So, why don't you explain the details of your relationship to me?"

"Will my husband find out?" I felt like such an idiot.

"Does it really matter?" The detective put his pencil tip down to the paper.

I sighed. If Todd really was a killer, they needed all the gory details.

"Okay, I'll tell you about Todd – and me."

12

Tuesday morning swim practice went like clockwork. Daniel was back. The team was in better spirits than they had been in during Monday's practice without him.

Determined not to mess the swim team up any further, I was firm without being bitchy. Everyone was there, but Todd.

I barely noticed John's presence. He didn't make a scene about "us." John was like every other member of the team. When I said swim, he swam. Although he still raced, when we weren't doing speed drills, just as he had on the first day of practice. Now that I knew John, I realized that it was more of a competitive thing, than it was an ego thing. He wasn't showing off. He was just being his best.

I couldn't help but watch him. His work ethic was commendable. John had a silent confidence. He didn't need to boast; his times spoke for him.

The times for the team overall were good – better than last weekend's meet. It was clicking. Maybe we could be winners. Maybe I could find happiness and success with this team.

After practice, I called Daniel over. He looked normal. If I hadn't known him, I would have never suspected that he had stopped breathing a mere three days ago.

"How are you?" I asked the boy whose shoulders were barely broader than my own.

"I'm good, Coach." Daniel smiled and looked on sheepishly.

"Don't be embarrassed about last weekend, Daniel. It wasn't your fault," I told him.

"Yes, it was, Coach. I took too many sleeping pills." Daniel admitted. He avoided my eye contact.

"You did? Why?"

"I don't know. I just wanted to sleep. And Todd is so weird... He kept playing those video games. It was so annoying. Please don't room me with him again."

"Your roommate was annoying you, so you OD'd on sleeping pills?" I tried to make sense of what he'd told me. It was beyond ridiculous. Was everyone around here a psycho?

"Um...yeah, I guess so. I'm sorry. Please don't put me with him next weekend."

"I won't. But, you have to promise me that you will never swallow another pill unless a Doctor specifically tells you to," I urged him.

"I promise," he said.

"Never again!" I repeated, angered by his lackadaisical attitude. I had given him CPR and he was acting as if it was just a bad night, like when a college kid drinks too much and gets a hangover.

"Never," he said.

"Never! You scared us! I had to breath for you!"

"I'm sorry," he said, "And, thank you – for breathing for me."

"You're welcome. I couldn't very well let you die, Daniel. We need you on this team." I smiled to let him know that I cared. He smiled back. I patted his shoulder and sent him on his way. Once I was alone, I went for a swim.

Every so often I would look up from my laps. In the back of my mind I hoped that John would appear on the side of the pool. He didn't, though. No one was going to appear and profess his love for me.

John was a young, attractive athlete. I had told him to back off and he had done just that. He was not a stalker and he did not love me, nor, did I, him. He was just a substitute for the love I was missing in my relationship with Craig – Craig, who had only said that he loved me when I started crying. It wasn't fair for me to drag John into the crossfire of my dysfunctional life.

Our little fling was over and I felt relieved about that. Cheating on my husband by fooling around with a member of the swim team was dangerous and fun, but a very irresponsible thing to do. True, it made me feel sexy. Sex with John had been hot – scorching hot. It just wasn't worth all the stress and potential pain attached. If I were single, though, I'd give up coffee, if it meant some extra nookie time with John.

I showered off and got dressed. Then, I pulled the picture that I had stolen of Craig and Elizabeth out of my pocket. They stood there on a grassy knoll, blue skies overhead; their arms around each other. My stomach felt sick. What did the picture mean?

Craig was such a well-liked man. Everyone *loved* him! I *loved* him. After our falling out on Sunday, I felt like such a schmuck. I wanted to patch things up with him and prove that I appreciated all the wonderful things he had done for me.

Conversely, if he had fed me a bunch of bologna about all the strings he had pulled and how he had done so much for me, yada, yada, yada, but he really was sleeping with another woman, then Craig was the jerk of the century.

Maybe Elizabeth had been stalking him. Yes, that would make him the good guy. He can't help who stalks him. The stalker theory would explain why she kept a photo of them together – a photo that I don't remember being taken at a location that I didn't recognize. I did notice that they had their wedding rings on in the picture. That was a point in Craig's favor.

It felt like déja vu walking across campus to Craig's office.

I strode past the coffee shop, without going in. Kamber could be in there, after all. I loved coffee, but I barely tolerated *Kamber*. She was not on the top of my list of favorite people. For all I knew she tried to help her boyfriend kill Coach Sutton.

I wondered what would happen to Todd. Was it all a misunderstanding? Or was he a cold-blooded killer? I wished Detective Frank had given up more details.

I quickened my pace, eager to speak with my husband.

"Coach!" *Oh crap!* I knew that annoying voice. I stopped in my tracks and gave up. There was no sense in trying to out-pace Kamber. She wasn't the type to give-up.

I turned to see her and didn't bother pretending to smile. She did, though. Her cheesy toothy smile made my skin crawl.

"Hi, Kamber," I said.

"Hi, Coach. How are you?"

"I'm doing fine. And you?"

"How do you think I am? My boyfriend is in Jail!" She threw her hands over her eyes and tossed her head forward.

"Still? I thought they would let him out on bail or whatever it is they do until they have enough evidence."

Kamber flipped her hair out of her eyes and looked at me to speak, "Yeah. I don't know what is going on. I just know that I haven't seen or heard from him since yesterday morning."

"Maybe you should call the detective guy." I offered a potential solution that didn't involve me.

"I did. He doesn't answer or call back," she exclaimed.

"That's too bad, Kamber. I actually have to go." I began to turn.

"Coach!" she grabbed my arm, "I need your help."

"How can I help? The last time I saw him he was leaving the jail with you – leaving." I tried not to sound panicked by her sudden gesture, though that's how I felt.

"You're his coach! Do something!"

"Doesn't he have parents? Maybe you should call them," I said, wanting nothing to do with her. Kamber was dangerous.

"I don't know their number, or their names."

"Sorry, I can't help you." I wanted to leave, but she was still holding my arm. "Can you let me go please?" I gave her a dirty look.

She began to loosen her fingers and I thought I was free. *I wish!* Just as my face began to relax, Kamber refastened her claws into my flesh and pulled me in close. Kamber was a Bully!

"You listen here," the bully spoke to me through clenched teeth, "I know all about you. I can ruin you. You better help me or I swear to God I will ruin your Goddamn life."

I twisted my wrist and pulled out of Kamber's death grip. "Look here, *Kamber*. I don't know who you think you are, but nothing you could say could ruin me. And trying to strong-arm me isn't going to get you the results you desire. I prefer more gentle forms of blackmail."

"That's not all you prefer, skank," Kamber stumbled backward and yelled profanities at me. She was purposefully trying to cause a scene.

I spoke to her calmly, "I am an adult, *Kamber*, and a teacher at this University. Disrespecting me in front of passers-by will do you more harm than it will do you good. I liked you better when you pretended to be nice."

"I liked you better before you fucked the swim team!" she screamed.

That got my blood pumping! I couldn't let myself touch her. I had to stay cool. My breathing purposefully slowed and deepened as a way to chill my hot blood. I really *did* try to stay calm.

I tried… but it didn't work.

The veins in my arms bulged through my skin.

Fuck it! I thought, giving in to my temper. I walked up to her face and spoke in a gruff voice. "Look Bitch, your boyfriend is a psycho, stalker, older-woman loving killer. He tried to get with Coach's wife and he tried to get with me. I doubt he got any further with her than he did with me. I don't give a shit what he told you or what you may have found out through your little news channels. If you don't back the fuck off of me and let this go, I will be the one ruining your life!" I poked her above her chest and backed her up. "You forget that I am the adult with the reputation and you are nothing but a nineteen year-old, snot-nosed reporter who will say anything to make a story. No one gives a shit what you say."

Kamber stared at me, wide-eyed and stunned. I think she had planned to be the one to do all the pushing. She underestimated my boundaries. Unlike other teachers, it turned out that I'm not afraid to touch students – male or female.

I lowered my voice and stepped back. "Stay out of my life," I told her and turned on my heels.

As I walked away, I half expected to feel her jump on my back and wrestle me down. But, she didn't. The bully had backed down.

In reality, Kamber probably could ruin my life with her words. Hopefully, I had stunned her into silence.

*****

When I reached Craig's office, I didn't feel like bringing up the photo. There had already been enough excitement in my morning. I craved for things to be normal – boring. *Boring* suddenly sounded so alluring! I wanted to take a quiet lunch with my husband and chit-chat.

Craig was on the phone, lounging at his fancy desk, when I popped my head in the doorway. He was laughing at something the person on the other side said. Craig's broad smile was part of his magnetism. His teeth were large and sparkling white. He couldn't help but draw others in.

He looked up as I gently tapped my knuckles on the open door. I smiled at him and batted my eyelashes.

He appeared surprised to see me. I couldn't tell if my showing up was a good surprise or an unwelcome one. He gave me a smile. It wasn't as big as when he had laughed a moment ago, but it still felt good.

I mouthed the word "lunch" as he continued on the phone. Craig didn't mouth anything back to me. After another minute, he hung up the phone and stood up from his state of the art, ergonomic king-sized leather chair. "Susan," he said in a pleasant tone, "This is a nice surprise."

"Is it?" I asked to make sure he wasn't just being polite. I doubted all of my moves with him as of late.

"Is it?" he asked me back.

"I came to ask you out to lunch," I said in my most casual of voices, as if I were just passing by his office with no ulterior motive.

"That's nice of you," he said, "But I have plans."

I waited for him to finish his statement. But, he didn't. That was all he said, 'I have plans.' He didn't offer up any extra information, like who his plans were with or what he was doing.

"Oh I see," I replied. I didn't want to play the suspicious wife role with him anymore. I would be suspicious when I was away from him and I would play it normal in his presence.

He walked over and gave me a formal hug, complete with three pats on the back, which I returned. When we broke our embrace, I told him that I had a lot of work that I could get done in my office in lieu of a lunch date.

"Okay, Suzy." He smiled at me, convinced that I would be just fine without his company, and leaned on the doorway.

"See you later, Craig." I blew him a desperate kiss and walked away. He smiled and walked back into his office, closing the door behind himself.

I wanted him to long for me, like he used to. But I had to play it cool and not get in his space. If I worked it right, I could get him back, I just knew it. What I needed was a plan.

But, as much as I hated it, I had to gather some intel first. I made a phone call and set the wheels in motion.

13

I sat down on the bench in the Cactus Garden at UNLV. When I made the phone call a few hours ago I thought that I would be nervous about meeting Todd in the spot where we had kissed a mere two weeks ago. But, I wasn't. I felt calm and focused.

I needed to get my life headed in the right direction. Todd could give me the answers I needed.

It didn't surprise me that he answered my phone call. He had obviously been avoiding Kamber, according to her tales. But, he was *my* stalker, so he would never avoid me - at least not until he found a new object of his infatuation.

I was the first to arrive, however.

Perhaps I overestimated his affections, I thought as my relaxed mood gave way to nerves. I sat. And I waited. My blood thickened. I could feel my heart work to pump the now dense liquid through the veins in my throat. Fifteen minutes passed before he showed his face in the warm afternoon sun.

Todd sauntered toward me; his casual gait appeared contrived. His tardiness was a control tactic. I didn't take it personally. He was a stalker who felt vulnerable. This was his way of trying to dig his claws back into me.

"Hello Todd," I greeted him.

"Hi," He didn't sit down or remove his dark sunglasses. He stood five feet away from the bench, which was perfectly fine by me. I wasn't trying to win Mr. Crazy back. I just wanted answers.

"So, they didn't keep you or anything?" I asked.

"Who?" His forehead wrinkled above his shades.

"The police. Kamber told me that you were being held at the station and she hadn't heard from you... blah, blah, blah."

"Oh. I, uh, I just told her that to keep her away for a bit. You saw me leave the police station."

"She was with you."

"Which is why I've been avoiding her," Todd stated in a tone that suggested what he really said was, "duh."

I changed the subject. "I'm guessing you are quitting the team, then."

"Why?" he asked innocently.

"You didn't show up to practice today. That says 'quitter' to me. You also didn't show up to my class, not that it really matters anymore. You are failing."

"I don't want to quit. But, I don't like the way that the guys - and you – look at me. They think I'm a killer." He sounded hurt. I could see his eyes to look for sincerity there.

"Are you?" I asked him.

"No!" He was adamant.

"Then, would you please explain to me what happened?"

"Daniel took those pills. I didn't give them to him." He crossed his arms.

I was getting pissed. I was sick of him being ambiguous and aloof. "Not Daniel! I was there for the Daniel incident. I saw that for myself! Coach Sutton, Todd! What happened to Coach Sutton? Tell me the story. I need to know the story!"

"There is no story." He looked away. He was holding back.

"There is, too. Tell me what you told Detective Frank."

"Nothing!"

"Tell me about Elizabeth! Tell me about the notes!"

"No," he began, "I can't tell you. I don't want to hurt you," he said, backing up.

"Get back here and sit down. You are not going to hurt me. I don't have feelings for you, okay?"

"God! You are full of yourself!" Todd exclaimed.

I stared at him. My mouth fell silent.

He stared back, then continued, "Susan, the story is a messy love triangle. But, knowing about Elizabeth and me… and another party involved would only hurt you."

I must have been having a really dumb day, because I had no idea who another party was. I shouldn't have pressed him, but I did.

"Just tell me," I directed him. My eyes bore into his like those an angry mother who had been drinking and now demanded answers from her weak child.

He hemmed and hawed and finally gave in. Todd took off the sunglasses, sat down and told me his story. "Okay, well I met Elizabeth through Coach. He was really into doing things together as a team to create comradery or something. We were always at his house for dinner. She smoked outside, so I would go out on the deck and talk to her. We began to get to know each other and things got – sexual."

"Wait – are you sure this wasn't just in your head?" I asked. He had told people that he things got sexual with me, too.

"Susan, I am telling you what I told the Detective. This is the truth."

"Okay. I'm sorry. Go on." I humored him, but I wasn't sure that I could trust what he said.

"Anyway, it started innocently with Elizabeth. But, as I said, it became more. We first kissed outside on the deck. Coach was right inside the house! It was flippin' hot! Soon, we started sleeping together."

I rolled my eyes. It reminded me of someone I knew, namely me.

"Seriously," he assured me.

"Really? Who called who?" I asked him, not bothering to hide my skepticism.

"She would call me and then come over to my apartment."

"Okay. Fine. So you wrote her a love letter? And that's what Kamber found?"

"No, I wrote her a rage letter," he corrected me. Then he cocked his head, "Wait? What? Kamber found that letter? I'm in this mess because of *Kamber*?"

"Um... Yes. I thought maybe you knew that." I felt uncomfortable knowing that I was the one who broke the rotten news of his girlfriend's traitorous act toward him.

"No, I didn't know." Todd's face turned many shades of red. I couldn't tell if he was embarrassed or angry.

"Calm down. She doesn't know who wrote it."

"You'd be surprised how much she knows." He muttered and began to stand up.

"Wait. Sit down. Why did you write Elizabeth an angry letter?"

"I caught her with another man."

"Well, she was married, Todd. How did you catch her? Were you stalking her? Texting her at all hours of the night? Leering through her windows?"

"It wasn't her husband that I saw her with. And, no, I wasn't stalking her. I stayed home from an out-of-town swim meet. I knew Coach would be gone, so I went to Sutton's house to surprise her. I knocked on the door, but no one answered. I started to walk away when I heard a familiar moan and a giggle coming from behind the house. I couldn't stand it. I had to know what was happening. So I snuck to the backyard and crept below the deck. As you can imagine I saw Elizabeth and *him* doing the nasty above me."

My stomach sank. I felt my heart begin to tear. "Who was it, Todd?"

"I didn't know who he was."

I breathed a brief sigh of relief. As the air left my lungs, I felt the enormity of weight of my heart thumping in my chest. "How does this affect me, then?"

"I saw *him* with you. *You* arrived at the funeral with *him* – the guy I saw fucking Elizabeth over my head. It was your husband."

I stared at him, silent for a moment.

"Shit," I eventually said. His final admonition was a screwdriver to my heart. It twisted and bled into my body with each heavy thump. How was that for karma? I was finally ready to fall back in love with my husband and now there was a fresh wound to repair - a deep gouging wound. I visualized blue blood seeping into the tissue below my ribcage.

"I thought you knew about it. I actually thought that you knew about everything – me, her, and *him* – and that was why you chose me to fool around with me - to get back at him."

"No. It wasn't to get back at him. I felt lonely and you were cute, attractive and there," I owned up to the petty selfishness of my recent actions.

"Huh," he processed what I said. I could see his brain turning over thoughts in his head.

"Huh," I repeated. My own mind turned itself off. It was too much. The story overwhelmed me. I didn't even know where to begin.

"That sucks," I told Todd, "I wish you hadn't told me."

"I tried not to tell you, but you're so pushy."

"Shut up." I turned away from him and took steady breath. My fingers trembled, but I was surprised to find that I didn't feel like crying.

A moment passed and I hoped Todd would leave. Instead, he tapped my shoulder and asked, "Am I still on the team, Coach?"

"What? Are you mentally unstable? How could you ask me that?"

"Is that a no?"

"I don't know. Who killed Coach Sutton?"

"Food poisoning killed him. He ate a bad piece of meat. I didn't do it."

"How long ago did you write that note to Elizabeth, Todd?"

"It was a few days before Sutton died. But, I had no reason to kill him. I think he was the only one *not* sleeping with his wife!"

"Maybe you did it to hurt her because she hurt you," I said, giving him a motive.

"What are you, LVPD? The detective cleared me and declared Coach's death an accident. So just lay off. I didn't do anything! Come on! Am I on the team or not?"

"Not." I told him.

"Why?"

"You said it yourself. Your teammates are uncomfortable around you and so am I. The proof is in the 'bitch' note you wrote to me. I don't want to be around you."

"But, I told you this whole story!" He whined like a five-year-old who wanted a toy he was forbidden to have.

"Please. You were dying to tell me about Craig, Todd. I'm sure you wished you could tell me ever since you realized that the guy was my husband. I saw the satisfaction in your eyes as you told me!"

"You are a bitch!"

"I know. I really am a bitch, Todd. But, I'll tell you what. I'll give you an, 'A' in my class and help you transfer to another school that has a swim team. It won't be a school in the same division as UNLV. But, you can walk on and do your thing."

"I don't want to walk on to another team! I want a scholarship."

"You'll just have to prove yourself during your walk-on year. Maybe they'll give you a full ride for the last two years. It's better than nothing."

He looked at me with sad, puppy dog eyes.

"I'm not going to change my mind. Say the word and I'll call a few schools and arrange it for you."

"This sucks," he sighed.

"I know. How about you don't show up to my class for the rest of the semester? Just send me an e-mail with your top three transfer choices and I'll help make it happen."

Todd tried the puppy dog eye thing once more. I didn't flinch as I stared back, my own eyes empty wells of transparent color.

"Okay," he finally said.

*****

I entered some grades for a recent speech that my students had given. When I got to Todd's name, I typed in an "A," just as I had promised. I didn't feel good about fudging his grade. It wasn't something I had ever done before; Nor was kissing a student and getting mixed up in Todd's mess of a life. But, his mess was my mess now.

I wasn't completely certain which of the terrible twosome (Todd or Kamber) was the real bad guy, or if either of them was *bad* at all, for that matter. But, some things in life just don't ever get completely resolved. I guessed that I would always wonder about the idiotic couple with whom I was tangled in the crazy poisoning mystery. But, I was so exhausted by them, that I didn't care to know the details of who did what to whom with what where anymore.

At that point I would have done just about anything to get that boy to switch schools. Todd was bad luck. He needed to go. Screw closure, I just needed him gone.

I think I got off easy – one free "A," plus a mid-year transfer. And the bonus was that no one was going to find out. Well – one person would have to be told. But, I would cross that bridge when I came to it.

When I finished updating my grade book, I picked up the phone. Up until this morning, I dreaded the thought of making this call. But now, nothing she could tell me would be a surprise. Psychologically, I was ready for anything, or, so I thought.

My determined fingers found her name in my contact list and hit send. She picked up on the second ring. I almost hit the hang-up button, but something stopped me. I had to do this.

"Hello?" she asked. The sound of her tired voice irked me. It was like listening to cat claws scratching glass.

"Hey, it's Susan."

"Susan? Uh, hi. How are you?"

"Well, Elizabeth. I've been better…I've been better." I hoped that the tone in my voice would give it all away. Maybe Elizabeth would realize that I was on to her little sexcapades and confess it all over the phone right then! *Go ahead, husband-fucker, spill. Tell me everything,* I tempted her via ESP.

No such luck.

"I'm sorry to hear that, Susan. Can I help you with something?" It was the syrup voice now. She was playing it cool. Elizabeth was going to make me drag it out of her.

"Yes. I think you can help," I kept that edgy tone in my voice. I wanted her to feel apprehensive. I wanted her to know that *I knew.* I needed her to belly ache out of stress and her skin to crawl out of disgust with herself!

I took a pregnant pause. I could hear her shallow breathing from her side of the phone.

"Can I come over?" I finally asked.

"Ummm, when?" She was stalling, I could tell, but she still sounded calm.

"Right now?" I asked.

"Now isn't good. How about tomorrow?"

Stall tactic! With my luck she would conveniently forget our meeting. But, I had no choice but to accept the offer.

I decided to dangle a carrot. "Tomorrow will do," I responded. Then I added, "And I hate to say this, but I must confess that I stole something when I was at your place last weekend."

"You stole something?" She coughed a bit.

"Yes. I'm sorry and I will return it tomorrow."

"What did you take, Susan?"

"I'll return it to you tomorrow. Goodbye." I hung up before she could reply.

*****

Craig was the last person that I wanted to ask about the whole Elizabeth love triangle thing. Literally, I had planned to ask him about it long after I had spoken with her.

I wrangled with it the entire way home. Part of me wanted to confront him and ask him for his side of the story. Maybe it was all just a big misunderstanding. After all, could I really trust Todd's word against Craig's?

Conversely, if Craig admitted to carrying on an affair with Elizabeth, could I forgive him? Worse than that, what if once he copped to it, he decided he had nothing to lose? What if he left me for her? It was the ultimate heartbreak, not to mention utter humiliation; learning that your husband loves someone else more than he loves you.

As I pulled my laptop bag out of the passenger seat, I concluded that I couldn't say anything to Craig. I simply could not let him find out that I knew anything about a past or present relationship between him and Elizabeth.

I resolved to love him. I could not allow myself to seek love in the arms of other men any longer. *It isn't what normal people do? Normal people seek love from their own partner, the one at home,* I told myself. That meant that I had to find a way to remind Craig that he loved me. Arguing over another woman would only push him into her arms. I needed him to choose me over the affair.

Puddles meowed when I came in through the garage door. I petted her furry little head and hung my bag in its assigned place in the entryway.

My nose hairs tingled. A luscious lemony scent came from the kitchen. I heard a scrubbing noise as I walk toward the odor, which become stronger and acerbic as I got closer. I entered the tiled room to find Craig on his knees. He was home early.

"You're cleaning!" I said, surprised by his actions. He made a mean sandwich and killer salads, but the man never cleaned; not with an actual sponge and water mixed with lemony ammonia stuff.

"Yes," he looked up and put the sponge in a bucket before stashing the supplies in the back corner of the room. His hands were covered with gloves. "I would hug you, but..." He gestured to his big, yellow cleaning gloves.

"You hate to clean," I observed, trying to read through the stoic and obvious lack of expression on his face.

"I did this for you. I wanted to make you happy," Craig replied. He sure had a way of making me feel like the bad guy lately.

"Really?" There was more than a hint of skepticism in my voice. What was he cleaning up and why was he home early?

As if he read my mind, Craig quickly changed his story. "Okay – I spilled something and tried to clean it up before you got home," he offered up as his real confession.

"What did you spill?" I asked.

"What did I spill?"

"Yes, what are you cleaning?"

"Milk, I spilled milk," he spoke resolutely. But, I knew him too well. He wasn't telling the truth. It was like a switch had been flipped and everything about him became completely transparent. There would be no more of my buying his dazzling smile and witty repartee. I saw through him. It was a frightening moment of clarity.

I had grown tired of his shit and I could no longer take what he said at face value. He needed to lay down his cards, so that I could show him my hand. If we both spoke frankly, cleared the air, then we could have a chance to start over.

"I wish I could believe you, Craig." I walked around the wet tiles still shiny from the citrus flavored cleaner and crossed to the counter where Craig's phone lay.

"What is wrong with you? I thought you would be happy that I am cleaning in such a thorough manner!" Craig said, eyeing me as I picked up his phone.

There were no incoming calls or outgoing calls. "You deleted your call log, Craig."

He took his gloves off and walked toward me. "It was full," he said, "I had to empty the calls to free up memory."

"I don't believe you."

"Then, tell me, Susan. *Who* do you think was in my call log? What do *you* think I am cleaning up?"

"Cum. I think you are cleaning up after having unprotected sex with Elizabeth Sutton in our kitchen! In our kitchen! Coach's wife. I think you fucked Coach's wife earlier!" This was an unplanned spill of words. At that moment I realized that did not want to have this argument. I didn't want hear the outcome – to hear my husband break up with me. But, it was too late. I was already in the moment.

He stared at me.

I felt the steam of rage begin to build inside me as I pushed at Craig for answers. "Were you? Have you? Are you sleeping with her?" I heard my voice crack.

"You're crazy," he said and walked out of the room.

"Get back here, Craig! You are fucking Elizabeth! You are fucking Elizabeth! You are fucking Elizabeth!" I kept screaming it, over and over. There were no thoughts in my head. Raw emotion took over: fury, fear and rage. *Rage! Rage! Rage!*

I kept screaming, like a broken record gone completely nuts.

Craig came back into the kitchen, his face was purple and his hand was up. Before I knew it, his hand smacked my jaw, open palm, and flung me to the ground. I landed on my ass and my hand with a thud on the tile floor.

"Shut Up!" he howled.

I slumped over. My jaw dropped. Thoughts flew around like witches on broomsticks playing Quidditch in my skull. I processed the current situation from my slumped over position on my ass. As the Harry Potters flew in circles, I fought to find my right mind.

I felt the damp floor through my pants and pried my palm from the ground rolling my wrist, which ached from catching much of my body weight.

He stood over me and glared at my bewildered face. "Yes, yes, yes! I slept with Elizabeth. I 'fucked' her, as you said. Are you happy?"

I didn't reply. I look up at the eyes that glared at me. He looked more like a rabid animal than a human. His eyes were wild and red.

He kicked my side and asked again, louder, "Are you happy, Bitch?"

"No!" I kicked him back, barely attacking his ankle from my position on the floor, and continued, "I am not happy! You are fucking someone else! You did it in our house! Without a condom!"

"Did you just kick my ankle? Who are you to kick me?"

Was he laughing? He spoke it a tone I had never heard from him before.

"Don't even try to kick me, Susan."

He kicked me again, harder, in the rib. We both heard the sound of it crack. I gasped. He didn't flinch. "You hear me, cunt? Don't you ever fucking try to kick me!"

Who was this guy? This was not who I married. This was a crazy monster. He was the wolf and I was the lamb. Only this time, he was going to kill me.

I grabbed onto a chair and made my way up to a seated position. "You hurt me, Craig!" I was involuntarily crying now.

"I hurt you? No! You hurt me! I never wanted you to find out about it, Susan. But, you just kept pushing and pushing."

"I thought something weird was going on," I explained.

"This is your fault," he howled like a man betrayed, "You pushed me into her arms. Then you had to find out about it. I could tell you knew I was up to something so I broke it off with her. You hear me?" He kicked the chair, "I broke it off with her."

I listened as I rested my face on the seat of the chair, softly letting out a whimper with each painful breath I inhaled.

"We were in love, Susan! Elizabeth and I were in love and I broke it off to protect you! Talk about hurt! It hurt Lizzie and me the most – to be apart!"

"Shut up, Craig," I cried with my head down, "It hurt you to be apart. Screw you. It's been, what? Hours?" I wasn't sure what pained me the most, my cracked rib, realizing that Craig was an evil monster or hearing that he was in love with Elizabeth out loud from his own mouth.

"I broke it off! I had broken it off! Then she called me today and said that you were on to us. She said that you threatened her and stole from her and she needed to be with me. She came over and we fucked, Susan. We did it all over this kitchen. Is that what you wanted to know? We did it on the table, the counter, the floor and in that chair where your face is!"

My face shot up from the chair. Craig's words got me. His nasty verbiage dug into me deeper than the aching in my ribcage.

He laughed at my knee-jerk reaction to his reveal. He circled me like an animal circles its prey. The wolf was deciding how to finish me off.

He stopped moving when he was behind my back and spoke in a creepy whisper, "Susan, you brought this on yourself. You wanted this. You wanted to know all this. So, there it is. The truth. Hurts, doesn't it!"

Yes, it did.

I used the chair and the table to stand all the way up and leaned on the nearby counter so I could watch his face react as I spoke. "You know what? Elizabeth was sleeping with someone else at the same time as she was with you, so fuck you, Craig. You got cheated on by the whore that you cheated with. You are a bastard - A fucking bastard!"

I leaned in and enjoyed a morose sense of satisfaction watching the man who had always kept so calm and collected boil over and contort in reaction to my revelation. It was as if some psychopath with feelings like a woman with PMS took over Craig's body. My emotional attachment to him was now severed and the need to kick his ass overtook me. I had to win this brawl.

"No, fuck you, bitch. You are a liar! Get out of my house!" He pushed my face back with the palm of his hand.

"It's my house too," I cried, "Go live with Elizabeth!"

"No! You go live with one of the boys on the team. Don't you know that I know about you? People talk, Suz! You're fucking the swim team that I put you in charge of! Slut!"

"I'm not leaving. I slid down the counter and pulled my knees to my chest." It was all so surreal. I had never in a million years thought this would happen to me, or that Craig would say or do such harsh things. Maybe his body really was possessed.

"Fine, I'll go." He picked up his phone and his briefcase and walked out the front door.

And just like that, he was gone.

I locked all the doors and put some ice on my face. I had a feeling that the wounds were going to leave a mark or two.

After a few hours of trying to sleep, I drug my tired body to the emergency room.

I couldn't look the clerk in the eye. Not because I was incapable, but because I felt ashamed. "What happened, Ma'am?" she asked.

I tried to explain what had happened to my face, but when I opened my mouth, .I could form no words. There was a huge guilt bubble in my mouth and it would allow no room for pronunciation.

I turned away. Speaking meant reliving what I desperately wished I could erase. It meant admitting guilt – his and mine.

So, I did the only thing I could do in that moment. I cried.

The woman came around from behind her desk, put her arm around me and helped me past the waiting room and to a bed behind a curtain.

I sat and sobbed as Nurses and Doctor came in and out of the curtain until my wounds were sufficiently dressed. They wrapped my waist, gave me ice for my face and told me to rest. The rib would heal on it's own.

I felt like vomiting.

'Did I want to press charges?' I think they asked.

"Ma'am?"

The room felt cloudy like a small bar full of chain smokers.

I was dizzy.

"Ma'am?"

There was a ringing in my ears.

"Ma'am?"

I didn't answer.

14

"What happened to your face, Coach? There is a purple mark on your left cheek," Daniel asked at practice. It had only been a few hours since I left the emergency room and I guessed that the bruise was more pronounced now.

Maybe I should have skipped it. But, all I could think was that practice was something normal I could do to remind myself that life does go on.

"I would really appreciate it if no one would ask me anything or say anything about my face today, okay?" I instructed the team as a whole.

There was no sense in wearing sunglasses. Much of my bruising was hidden beneath my shirt. I had tried to conceal my face with make-up. But, that only did so much.

The boys had a meet coming up this weekend and I prayed that my war wounds would be gone by Saturday. It was so embarrassing. This was worse than the time that Craig had left a huge hicky on my neck after a passionate night of lovemaking. That would have been five years ago. I hadn't even noticed the lovebite, then, but my students sure did the following day.

The Craig who used to make passionate love to me was a person who existed only in my distant memories now. He was replaced by the crazy monster, who had called me the C-word. I had never in my whole life heard someone say that word out loud. Sure, I had heard it in the movies and from comedians doing stand-up, but never in real-life.

I hardly noticed the boys swimming, as I ran through last night events over and over in my head. The first hit had been shocking, but I still couldn't believe that Craig kicked me. *He kicked me more than once!* This was not the man that I married. I couldn't rationalize how I could have spent so many years married to someone and not even know who he truly was. What else didn't I know about him?

I was staring off into outer space, when John spoke to me. It was too soon for him to be out of the water. "Coach?" he asked.

"Get back in the water, John. We're not done with practice."

"Actually, we are, Coach."

"What?" I looked around at the empty pool deck. The team was gone.

"I cut the practice short and sent the guys to the locker room."

"Oh. Then, you can go, too, John."

"Gee, thanks, Susan. But I think I'll stay a sec. Are you okay?"

"Yes." I didn't even try not to sound bothered by his foolish question, "I told you not to ask."

"I don't need to ask. It's written all over your face." John lightly ran a finger along the edge of my bruise.

"Ha, ha," I smiled at his pun. His touch felt good, even to my raw face.

"Do you need help, Susan?" John was genuinely concerned. I could see it in his soft brown eyes.

"I'm fine, John," I assured him.

"You don't look fine. If that bastard ever touches you again, I swear to God, I'll-"

"You'll nothing," I cut him off, "because he is gone."

"Are you sure? You're not in any danger?"

"Yes, he moved out last night. I watched him leave."

"Really? He moved out? All in one night?" John asked.

"Yes. I mean he didn't take any of his stuff with him, but, John, I'm fine. Bruised ego and shattered dreams is all."

"I feel like this is all my fault." He took my hand in his and lightly stroked my fingers.

"It's not on you. That wasn't what it was about at all."

"Are you sure? Because if I found out that my hot wife was with a sexy Latino guy like me, I'd-"

"John! That wasn't what it was about."

"Okay."

"So, you can rest easy tonight knowing that you didn't cause this," I motioned to my bruise, and added with a weak smile, "You think I'm hot?"

"Baby, you are en fuego! I would be proud if you were mine, bruises and all. I mean I'd have to put a tracking device on you," he teased me.

I lightly tapped him with my fist. It was still tender from landing on it last night.

"You should go home and rest," John advised. He was right.

"I have a class," I said.

"I'll put a 'class cancelled' sign on the door for you. What's the room number?"

"CBC 408."

"Fourth floor? Nevermind. That's too many stairs," John joked. He made me feel better just by making light of things. Maybe life could go back to normal once the bruises subsided.

"Thank you," I told him.

"No problem. You go home, okay?"

"Okay."

"And change the locks. You don't need him coming back and surprising you."

THE HOUSE SMELLED LIKE RUSTY SOUR LEMON WHEN I ENTERED. I was going to take John's advice and get some rest. In all the commotion last night, I hadn't poured out the bucket Craig used to clean up his sex mess. I didn't want to touch it now, either. Quite frankly, I was never planning on going into the kitchen ever again.

My plan was to grab the cat and a suitcase and lay low at the nearest hotel.

Instead, I took some Ibuprophen and lay down on the couch with Puddles. We were pooped. I did my best to push away all the horrible flashbacks. I turned on the television and eventually fell asleep to a *Friends* rerun.

I slumbered for about four hours and slept pretty soundly. My body was attempting to heal some of its wounds.

Puddles pawed at me and I tried to subdue her with a few pats. My eyes clenched closed, unready to return to the reality of my shattered life and badly bruised body.

Puddles had a different plan, however. She wanted food. I guess I had forgotten to feed her this morning and possibly last night. I searched my memory, but I couldn't recall whether or not I had fed my little furry pet. She was my only friend. I made a mental note to treat her better in the future and rolled off the couch. *So much for never entering the kitchen again!*

My body felt stiff as I made my way back to the scene of the crime. The kitchen was empty. Aside from the bucket in the corner, there was no evidence that my husband and I had engaged in warfare on the eve of today.

I grabbed some frozen peas out of the freezer and held them to my face as I wandered over to Puddle's water bowl. I picked it up and refilled it for her. She sat next to it and stared at me expectantly.

I picked up her food bowl and noticed some blood on the edge. It seemed a bit out of place. I hadn't bled when Craig struck me last night. Plus, I wasn't near the cat bowl when I fell.

I set the bowl on the counter and got a fresh one out for Puddles. She meowed to let me know that I could feed her anytime. I poured an entire can of turkey and gravy cat food into her bowl as a peace gesture. She accepted it and began licking all the gravy off of the meat morsels.

I didn't want to stay in the kitchen, but I felt that I had to check it out. Fear of what I would find made my hands tremble. After what happened last night, I was well aware that Craig was capable of anything. I was not safe. No amount of swimming or working out would help a woman defend herself against a strong man over six feet tall. Anyone could hurt me physically. I felt vulnerable.

I could only protect myself against the mental stuff. I defended my mind by blocking all the bad images out.

I checked out the floor and the table. It looked clean. There was a little smear of blood on the chair that I rested my face on last night. Nothing seemed out of place. Maybe the blood on the cat bowl was mine after all.

I picked up the bucket filled with a lemony ammonia cleaning fluid and poured it down the sink. I stopped when I noticed how dark the liquid was. I wondered if I was being paranoid as a result of being beaten up by the one person whom I always thought would protect me. But, I couldn't help but wonder if there was blood in the bucket?

I stopped mid-pour and placed the bucket on the counter.

What had Craig done?

I had hoped that I could just forget about the whole incident last night. I hadn't reported it to anyone because I didn't want to anger Craig further. Plus, what if no one believed me? He was very well liked, after all. It seemed that this whole thing was not going to disappear as quickly as my bruises would. I had to call Detective Frank.

Frank arrived within the hour. I was waiting for him on the front porch. My sunglasses didn't fool him.

"Yikes!" the detective said as he walked up to the house. "I think I can guess what you wanted to show me," he said in a pompous tone. I wanted to hit him in the jaw just as hard as Craig had hit me the night before.

"This isn't what worried me, Detective." I showed him inside. Puddles was waiting inside the door, but she ran and hid when she saw the detective's unfamiliar shoes.

I explained to him how I found Craig cleaning when I got home last night and gave him the play-by-play of the hideous blowout where Craig kicked the crap out of me. When I was done reliving it, I was certain that I never ever wanted to tell the story out loud again. I felt as if my insides were on display for all to poke at and see, revealed for what they really were – black and corroded, like the lungs of a smoker.

The detective took a few pictures and swabbed the places where I thought there was blood. He grunted and mumbled a few things that I couldn't make out. He wandered around some more and took a few more photos. I retired to the couch as he checked out the rest of the house.

"Okay," he said, walking back downstairs, "I'll take this to the lab and give you a call. Don't do anything to the kitchen, like clean or move things, okay?"

"Yeah. Sure."

"Bye," the detective mumbled coldly as he shut the door behind himself.

"It's been swell, Detective," I called out to the closed door.

And that was it. I had expected a big dramatic scene with cops and CSI guys. But, Detective Frank grunted around for less than thirty minutes and left swiftly.

It must have been nothing. The blood must have been mine. I felt dumb for having called him over. He didn't even ask me where Craig was. Not that I knew.

I stayed on the couch and turned on the television, again. It crossed my mind that I understood why Daniel had taken the sleeping pills. Maybe his life sucked like mine did. I found another *Friends* rerun and closed my eyes. At that moment I wanted to fall asleep and never wake up.

Puddles curled up next to me. I tried so hard to sleep, but I couldn't shut my mind off. The imagery kept replaying itself over and over. Each time I would visualize myself fighting back harder, but even in my own imagination, Craig would end up beating me to a pulp in the end. Was I sick in the head? Why couldn't I make the bad memories stop?

I gave up and called Daniel. He could make all the bad visions disappear.

He arrived soon after we hung up. "Is this a test?" he asked me, walking through the front door I left unlocked.

"Whoa!" He stood still in the foyer as I turned to face him from my nest of blankets and cat fur.

"No, Daniel. It is not a test. Look at my face. I just want to sleep until the bruises disappear and I forget this ever happened. So, what do you have? I'll take it all."

"I don't know, Coach." Daniel looked me up and down.

"Please Daniel. I was kidding about the 'take it all thing.' You know? Like, 'ha ha my face hurts and I want to die.'"

He gave me the one-eye glower.

I leaned forward. "Please. I promise to be responsible. I'll only take one."

"Okay," he took a bottle out of his pocket, "Here." He put one pill in my hand.

"That's it?" I asked like an ungrateful child.

"You just said, Coach. You said you would only take one," he stammered in a low voice.

"Today. I'll only take one today. But, I'm going to need a few for the rest of the week. Please, Daniel. I need your help. I really, really, really, really, *really* need this." I sounded like a junkie trying to get a fix. It was my last resort. I was going to take the pills or go suck on my car's tailpipe. One way or another, the pain would go away and I would sleep.

"Coach, I want you to feel better, but I think you should call me tomorrow. If you still want another pill, I will give you another one." He played the overprotective parent role well. I looked at him crossly, a spoiled brat who couldn't get what she wanted.

"Tomorrow? You'll give me more tomorrow?"

"I swear," he said.

"You are a good boy, Daniel."

"I know." Daniel studied me a moment. I was a picture of a woman unraveled. I pitied him. He must have been so uncomfortable. "Coach?" he asked.

"Yeah?"

"What about our meet?"

"I think your new Assistant Coach will have to go with the team to the meet."

"We have an Assistant Coach?" he sounded hopeful.

"Ummm. Not exactly. Not yet, but I will find you one by the meet."

"Really?"

"Yes. I'll make some calls today."

"Okay. Great, Coach, great. Maybe wait until after the calls to take that pill," he suggested.

"Good idea."

Daniel left and I got to work. I wasn't sleeping, but at least finding an Assistant Swim Coach gave me something other than last night to think about. I made some calls to my contacts at the University Athletic Department and found out some of the rules. They gave me the green light to choose whomever I wanted as assistant swim coach.

Finding an assistant was much easier than I had thought it would be. There were plenty of University Swim team Alumni in the area. Human Resources would do all the paperwork for the person of my choice. I just had to give them a name and send the lucky guy over to their office. Why hadn't I done this sooner?

It only took a few calls to find my guy. His name was Kent Clarkson. He had a deep voice and a level head. He was a Real Estate agent with a flexible schedule. Human Resources wouldn't be able to put him on the payroll officially until next week. So, I told him that this week would be his interview. He would go to the practices and oversee the meet on the weekend. I would transfer my plane ticket over to his name. If it all went smoothly, he was in.

"Great," Kent said in his smooth baritone voice, "I'll see you at practice tomorrow, Coach."

"Actually, it's just going to be you this week," I didn't know a good way to tell him why I wouldn't be there, so I made something up. "I was in an accident last night."

"Oh!" he sounded shocked.

"It's okay. I'm fine. Just a bit bruised up. I'll be back next week," I assured him. "Do you think you can handle them on your own for now?"

"Sure. I will take care of your team." Kent said.

"Our team," I corrected him and added, "thank you, Kent." He had no idea how he was bailing me out here. I hoped I would be up to facing the world again next Monday.

"You're welcome."

We hung up and I went to find the pill I had set down somewhere in the house. My brain was on overload today.

I stopped by the window. Craig's car was out front. *Shit! What now?*

I surveyed the area through the pane of glass and didn't see him. He didn't appear to be inside or anywhere around the vehicle. My eyes swept the front yard. Nope. Not on the grass or in the ugly cactus garden.

It felt wrong. A bead of sweat ran down my brow. The room swayed like I was on a boat. I cocked my head right and pressed my cheek into the glass. The driveway came into view.

There he was walking up the concrete drive. I swore I heard him whistle.

That fucked up Bastard!

I bolted to the front door and locked it. My heart beat triple time. My lungs expanded in and out, pounding against my tender ribcage.

I continued my sprint through the house, checking all possible entryways – windows, the sliding door to the back yard, the cat door.

The phone rang and I jumped sky high mid-run. I ignored it and raced to lock the back door. Not that it mattered. Craig had a key. Somehow I felt like I was buying time by turning the locks.

I turned the key, temporarily securing the back door and ran through the kitchen.

Then, I saw it - the butcher block. A knife was missing. Did Craig have it? Should I grab one? I didn't have the slightest idea which knife to grab or how to use it if it came down to it.

The phone rang again.

I abandoned the knives and went to the china hutch. Throwing my entire body weight at it, I attempted to push the antique forward. It moved about an inch and I felt as if my insides were bleeding. I needed to get it to the front door.

Craig's keys jingled outside.

Where was Puddles? I pleaded to no one in particular that the monster would not find my pet and hurt her.

I turned my back to the wooden furniture and pressed again. I grunted, panted and pushed more. It was moving.

The key was in the lock.

I looked around the large object, which was off of its wall and floating like an island in the hallway. There was no time. I had to leave it. He was going to open the door.

The phone in my pocket buzzed.

I picked up the phone as I leapt up the stairs. Adrenaline coursed through my body. I moved swiftly, as if none of last night's injuries had ever been inflicted.

I heard a squeak as the deadbolt lock turned in the front door. My feet quickly took me to my bedroom, where I shut the door in slow motion and tried to turn the lock without making noise.

"Hello?" I whispered, pressing the talk button on the phone.

"Susan? It's Detective Frank Buster. We found something."

"He's here," I whispered, begging into the receiver.

"There was blood in your kitchen that did not belong to you." He wasn't listening to me.

I could hear Craig moving around in the kitchen. He called for Puddles. I wondered if he knew I was home.

"He's here in the house, Detective!" I whispered. I could hear the rattling of cupboard doors being opened and closed. A drawer or two rolled out. It was hard to keep it straight as my ears began to ring.

"What? Who?"

"Craig. Craig is in the fucking house and he is going to kill me if you don't get over here right now!" I screamed under my breath!

The floorboards of the stairs creaked. *Shit!* I thought, about to have a heart attack.

"I'll be right there." The Detective hung up.

I crouched down behind the bed, listening to every step he took. He walked deliberately slow, as if he was trying to prolong my agony and draw out the torture.

I peered over the bed. The doorknob turned to right. Then it turned to the left. It began to alternate from side to side, faster and faster.

"Susan?" Craig asked, as if it were any day and I had accidentally locked him out.

I said nothing, frozen in fear. The ringing got louder in my head, threatening to explode though my holes.

"Susan, I need my clothes." He knocked on the door.

My eyes fixated on the door. I didn't dare take a breath, lest the painful ring come out of my ears and fill the room.

"Susan. You kicked me out, remember?"

He was acting like it was just some regular break-up. Craig spoke like we had had a normal married couple-type argument, which led to my kicking him out. Had he forgotten about smacking me to the ground and kicking me once I was down?

The ring numbed my ear drums and thumped at my brain. It sent my mouth open wide. "I kicked you out?" I couldn't stop myself. "I didn't kick you out. You beat the shit out of me, remember?"

"Susan. Don't be irrational. I always thought that if we broke up, you would be levelheaded about it. You're not one of those crazy exes that throws her husband's clothes on the lawn."

"You are shitting me! Why would I be the crazy one? You threw me around the kitchen like a rag doll! You are the fucking psychopath, Craig. You!" He gave me a good idea, though. I opened the window and went to his closet. As he continued to talk down to me, I tossed all his suits out the window, followed by his underwear and sock drawers. When I was done, I told him that everything he wanted was on the lawn.

"Are you kidding? Goddamnit, Susan. Not you. You wouldn't do this." His tone suggested his own belief in his innocence. The ringing started again, this time accompanied by the taste of vomit.

"Just go to the lawn. You'll find your stuff."

I heard the stairs creak rapidly as he ran downstairs. I watched the lawn, wondering where the cops were. *Detective Frank should be here by now.*

I just starred at his stuff strewn across our yard. *Cue the Knight in Shining Armour!*

Nope. Nothing. No knight and no Craig.

I anxiously tapped my fingers on the windowsill and looked from left to right.

Then, from the shadow of the downstairs overhang, he appeared.

Craig calmly walked to the lawn like any other guy whose psycho ex had thrown his stuff on the lawn. He gathered his suits up in his arms and walked the pile to his car, where he threw it in the backseat. Then, he returned for the rest.

I stayed in the window. I was not coming out until I knew he was gone. Craig would never hurt me again. I would find a way to make sure of that.

Craig looked up at me. "Can you at least throw down some of my toiletries?" he asked annoyed.

I went to his cabinet and got his favorite cologne and threw it at him. I hit him in the shoulder. It felt fantastic!

"Ow!"

"Fuck you, Craig!"

I ran back to bathroom to grab more heavy things to throw at him. Yes, the shampoo bottle! That should leave a mark.

When I returned to my battle station the enemy was no longer there.

There was no knock this time. Just a loud thud and Craig's red face staring me down as the door to our bedroom came falling toward the window, the bed and me. It hit the bed and bounced once before finding it's resting spot.

The ringing in my head pumped wildly. It was louder than whatever Craig was saying as he walked toward me with his arm extended.

His fist spread out, splaying his fingers around my neck. He lifted me upward. My hands automatically went up to his. I was a chicken about to become a meal. My feet dangled, helpless and weak. I cursed myself for provoking the beast.

The beast smacked my skull into the windowpane a few times before I felt it crack beneath my hair.

I attempted to suck in air as I felt my whole body thrown to the bed, my ankle hitting the sharp edge of the door.

I cursed myself again.

I could feel pressure against me.

The ringing continued. I began to see white.

The pressure worsened. And my nostrils and mouth began to suffocate.

The white became whiter.

The pressure got heavier.

Then, it stopped.

I disappeared.

And then there was sound. I could hear it through the pounding of the ring.

There was a voice.

Then there was more than one voice.

No pressure, just sounds. I could hear muffled voices and … *a squash being smashed?*

And breathe.

I breathed in.

And the fog of white began to lift.

And I could see the ceiling. I stared overhead as the ringing lessened. The sounds of voices became clearer to me.

"Susan?" John's enlarged black pupils came into focus. I felt his large hands lightly trace my jaw. He was the best thing I'd ever seen. A brown latin angel sent to protect me.

"You," I managed to say. *My knight.*

"No, just impeccable timing," he said.

I started with the questions only to be shushed with the lightest kiss from the softest lips that I couldn't have been happier to feel in that moment.

"That Detective just got here."

I could hear someone reading Craig his rights in the background.

Detective Frank appeared in the doorway. I turned my head to face him.

"You okay?" he asked. It was out of character for him to care, I thought. But, then I noticed that he wasn't really looking at me. All was normal. He didn't really care. The detective just wanted to arrest Craig.

"I'll be fine."

"Great,' He went on, "We learned a lot from the samples I took,"

"What did you find?" John asked.

"Well, for one thing, no one had sex in your kitchen last night."

"What? But Craig said –" I tried to raise myself to my elbows.

"He lied...the blood on the cat bowl belonged to Elizabeth Sutton."

"How could you tell? Did she give you, like a DNA sample or something?"

"Yes. Susan, she's dead." The Detective told me this with caution. He studied my reaction.

I was stunned. I never thought Craig was capable of murder. At that moment I learned the most important life lesson that I would ever take with me: You can never really know anyone.

"We found her in the park at the end of this subdivision. Craig didn't exactly do a good job covering this up," the Detective explained.

My world was officially flipped. *Had I gotten her killed? Could I have stopped it? Was she alive or dead hen he left last night?* How would I ever set it right?

The detective seemed satisfied with the look of shock and horror on my face and began to open all my drawers.

"What are you looking for?"

"I'll let you know when I find it."

"Maybe I can help," I offered.

"You can't."

I frowned.

"Look, the details of the what happened aren't important, Mrs. Templeton."

"Don't call me that," I cringed at the sound of his last name.

"The important thing is that, your ex is in custody, Susan."

There was a knock on doorframe. I jumped. John wrapped me in his arms and held me. Clearly, I was not okay.

Detective Frank let in another inspector type guy. He was wearing gloves and held something. "I found it," he said.

"What is that? A garden shovel?" John asked.

"It's a carving knife."

"Why is it covered in dirt?"

"It was dropped in the side garden," the inspector guy said.

"It's the murder weapon," Detective Frank explained.

John held me tighter and I broke down. There were tears and sobs and moans. He brushed my wet hair from my face.

The detectives looked him over with suspicion. "I'm a friend of Susan's. She's my swim coach," John said.

Detective Frank grunted and went back to bagging the knife. I continued to sob. Everything hurt.

John stroked my wet, knotted hair gently. He was just what I needed, a big strong person to lean on and make it okay.

After much more searching, endless talking and a never-ending argument with paramedics about not going to the ER, the circus of official people finally left.

"You can go, if you want," I said, "I know it's been a long and, uh, weird night."

John smirked and picked me up, as though I weighed that of a feather. He carried me to one of the spare bedrooms and placed me on the down comforter. My head sunk into the cloud of pillows.

He lay in bed next to me, his forehead inches from mine. John's soft eyes and heavy breath soothed me. I reached a hand out and fingered the emblem around his neck.

"What's this?"

"Saint Christopher. My Grandma gave it to me before I left for College."

"The Saint of travel."

"Yes. It's the last thing she gave to me."

"Oh. I'm sorry."

"Don't be. She was awesome." He smiled as if he were reliving a memory of her in his head.

The three of us slept cuddled together. John spooned me and I spooned Puddles.

15

"Welcome Back!" Daniel about jumped on me when he saw me Monday. He wagged around like an excited Golden Retriever puppy. It felt good to be greeted in such a way.

"Thanks," I smiled, "you're wet." I pulled at the back of my shirt where Daniel had left a watermark. He smiled back and returned to the pool to finish his laps.

I was relieved to have the team in my life. My bruises had faded and I felt confident to go out in public now.

I got the team out of the pool, so we could have a talk about their new Coach, Kent. They had nothing but great things to say about him. He was someone the boys could look up to. Plus, he was male. It was a perfect fit. I smiled.

I couldn't bring myself to go to their meet on Saturday. But, John stopped by my house for a visit upon his return and told me the same things about Coach Kent that the team was telling me now.

John was there for me last week. He was younger, but he was a rock. Somehow, he knew just the right amount of support to give without making me feel smothered. His company was just enough to keep me feeling safe.

In the aftermath of learning that my husband was a cold-blooded sociopath killer, I had contemplated quitting the team, resigning from UNLV and going home to Pennsylvania. Last night, John and I talked out the pros and cons. So, I got out of bed early this morning and came to practice. *Okay* – John pushed me off the couch. I hadn't been able to sleep in my bed since the Craig incident.

"That's so great that you guys like Coach Kent. Shall we keep him?" I asked the boys.

"Of course!" Daniel spoke up for the group.

"Great! Now get your asses back in the water. We have work to do." I smiled as I said this, so the boys would know that I was back, full of sarcastic remarks and ready for action. I didn't know how much they knew about what happened to me just over a week ago, but I didn't want them to worry about me, or, worse, to pity me.

"What did I miss?" asked the baritone voice I had spoken with only on the phone. Kent made his presence known and put out his hand to shake mine. "You must be Coach Templeton," he said in his warm low voice, "I'm Kent."

His stature and look matched his voice. He was a tall, handsome chocolate brown man. I felt myself blush. (Some things never change.) Hopefully he didn't notice the extra rouge appear in my cheeks.

"Its Susan, but how about we just call each other 'Coach?'" I said, returning his handshake with a smile. Kent's positive energy flowed from his fingers to my flesh and I knew that the team would head in the right direction with him at the helm.

"Sure, Coach," he told me.

"I hear that our team kicked ass last weekend at the meet." I gave him the recognition he deserved.

"Yeah," he said, "You have done a great job with them."

I could have disagreed with him, but instead I took the compliment. Maybe, there was some validity to it. Perhaps, I did do a good job with the guys, in spite of all my self-defeatist behaviors. I smiled at the thought and briefly forgot about the fact that my husband was being held in jail for the murder of his mistress.

I hoped that those moments of forgetting would eventually lengthen into segments, and then hours. Soon days would pass before I thought of it. I looked forward to that moment; the moment when I would realize that it has been days since I thought about my brutal two-faced ex-husband.

I watched the boys swim. Coach Kent directed the drills. With all these great people in my life, it was inevitable that I would one day barely recall what it was like to be married to a murderer.

After practice, I smacked John with a towel. He took it from me and used it to dry himself off. "Should I be worried?" he asked me as he toweled his hair.

"About what? Me?" I had no idea what he was referring to.

John gestured toward Coach Kent, who was across the pool talking to Daniel about something. "I saw you blush," he told me.

"Oh, that." I turned red at the thought of blushing. "That's just because I'm in my thirties. Handsome men trigger an involuntary bodily response. It happens all the time," I told him.

He frowned.

"I mean to say that I blush when I see a good looking guy, but it doesn't mean that I am interested. Trust me, I'm not interested in spicing up my love life for quite a while."

"Really?" John asked me. We hadn't had sex since before Craig had tried to finish me off, but he had held me in his arms until I fell asleep. He had stroked my hair when I awoke at midnight in a cold sweat. He had brought me coffee when I drug my feet in the morning.

"I don't know where we're headed, John. But, I trust you. And I appreciate your friendship and the fact that you have been here for me."

"But..." he looked into my eyes.

"No 'but.' I have no expectations for us. I don't want to jump back into having crazy college sex with you right away."

"Do you ever want to?"

"I have a lot of being on my own to do. But, you are a good friend, John. I wouldn't have had the courage to come back to coach the team without your support. For that I thank you."

"You're welcome," he said. John gave me a convincing smile and headed off to the locker room. I knew that was it for him. He wouldn't be calling me or coming over anymore.

I couldn't stand to watch him walk away. It broke my heart to shoot him down. He was basically everything I wanted in a partner. Sex with John was exciting, he was easy on the eyes, to put it lightly, and he was someone I could count on. But, the timing was all wrong. Could I start a serious relationship with a man so young, so soon after my husband killed his secret lover and attempted to kill me?

I wanted to call his name and have him run back to me and hold me in his arms.

"They are a good group," Coach Kent said, walking over to my side of the pool.

"Yeah. I think I'll keep them," I responded.

"Okay. I'll see you tomorrow," Coach Kent said, but I barely heard him.

"Yeah. Tomorrow," I mumbled, focused on the closed door to the locker room where John had just disappeared.

My head dropped and I stared at the floor as I walked out of the pool. I felt like I was doing everything wrong. Tears crept into my eyes. I didn't want anyone to notice, so I continued to look down as I quickly made my exit out of the building.

When I made it to my car, I let it out. The tears spilled from my eyes and a moan escaped my throat. I thought about everything. What had I done to deserve such pain and heartache? Was it my infidelity? Should I regret having gotten together with John in the first place? No. Had I not felt those feelings of unrest and sought to fix things, albeit in many unfaithful ways, I would never have snuffed out Craig for the rat that he was.

I continued to bawl. I was angry with Craig and angry with myself. How could I not have seen him for who he was? I felt foolish and stupid for having trusted such a horrible person. What was worse was that I didn't even miss Craig. I was glad he was gone, but upset over the horrific events that led to his exit from my life. Couldn't he just have cheated and left me like most men? Why did he have to kill and beat those who got in his way?

I thought about John again. He had been my rock through this. Was it possible that he felt the same way that I realized I had felt about him the moment he walked away this morning? I loved being with him.

It was silly, I know. He was supposed to be a safe fling to make me feel better about myself. John did make me feel better. He made me feel whole inside. It hurt to think that I would see him at practice from afar, but never be close to him again.

I tasted a tear on my tongue. *Stop being so pathetic*, I scolded myself.

It was time to suck it up and go it alone. I was going to have to get over John and pick up the pieces of my life.

I put the car in drive and went to the police station.

16

He was drinking coffee from an off-white, "World's Best Dad" mug. His crossed ankles rested on top piles of files, folders and papers on his desk. Detective Frank Buster was staring at the paper in his hand. Although, he may have been sneaking a nap. It was tough to tell from where I stood outside the office window.

I stepped into the doorway. He didn't acknowledge my arrival.

I cleared my throat and the old guy looked up. "Did I call you in Mrs. Templeton?" I cringed at the sound of my name. I no longer wanted to be *Mrs. Templeton.* I didn't want anything to connect me with that bastard, Craig.

"No. I came on a whim." My fingernails curled into my palm.

"Its hardly a whim. You're husband killed someone."

"Please don't call him my husband." My nails dug deeper.

"Well, you are married to him."

"Not for long." This was not going well. And I felt as if my nails were breaking my skin apart.

The Detective took a sip of his coffee and refocused on the paper he still held. *What a jerk!*

"Detective?"

He said nothing as his eyes moved horizontally across the text he was hell-bent on reading.

"Detective!" I said in a forceful voice. A passerby's head jerked toward the world's best dad's window. I swung to face him and he turned away swiftly, walking in the opposite direction.

"What?" He didn't even look up. I shouldn't have expected him to.

"I need your help."

"What now?"

"I need answers. And you could at least pretend to care." I put my hands on his desk. They slipped on all the papers and I recoiled before I fell face first into his mess.

"Answers?" he grunted and gave me a look that I couldn't understand.

"Yes. I can't put all the pieces together." I began to pace back and forth in his tiny office.

"Toots, you married a guy who killed the woman that he had been seeing behind your back. He probably – could you please stop that?"

"What?"

"Stop pacing. You're making me nauseous."

"Sorry." I stopped walking back and forth and stood still. There was no chair for me to sit in. *The douche bag doesn't have a guest chair on purpose! What a jerk!*

"Where was I? Uh, yeah, he probably killed her husband too. And there may have been others. Who knows?"

"Others?" I felt faint. I needed a chair. It just kept getting worse. "Detective, you're telling me that my husband killed Coach Sutton, Elizabeth Sutton and 'others?' Who else would he have reason to hurt?"

"Probably," the detective spoke so matter-of-factly. "Before he cheated with the Elizabeth Sutton, he probably fooled around with someone else. You never even suspected him of any of this? I'm guessing that you'll be piecing the mockery that was your life back together for quite a while." He stared me down from his side of the desk, daring me to stay and hear more.

"You act like I'm some stupid twit."

He nodded.

"Craig is a sociopath. You said it, yourself. I couldn't have seen it. Most trusting people wouldn't see through that façade."

"Did I say that?" He picked up a pencil and underlined a word on that stupid paper he had been reading.

"Yes. And you could try and be a bit more empathetic. This is very difficult for me to deal with."

"I'm not a therapist, Mrs. – Susan."

"Fuck!" I said to the Universe. "Nevermind," I said to him as I gave up and turned to leave.

"You never even asked your question," Detective Frank said with annoyance.

I took that as an invitation and turned back to face him. Words wouldn't form in my mouth, then. It was my big chance to get some questions answered. My mind went blank. I was blowing it!

I began to pace in his office. *What did I want to know?*

"Susan?" he asked.

I said nothing, only walked up and down. Four feet up. Four feet down. Four feet up. Four feet down.

Four feet up. Four feet down.

"Susan?"

Nothing.

"Susan. I have a gun. Ask your question or leave. And for God's sake stop pacing. It's making me want to shoot myself."

Right… a gun…Ah hah!

"What exactly happened that night?" I asked him.

"Which night? The one where he broke your rib or the one where he broke down your bedroom door?"

"The first night. The one where he was cleaning and then turned into a monster? I am unclear. Did he beat me up and them go kill her? Did he kill her then beat me for dessert?"

"It's pretty straight-forward, Susan. I think you already know this."

"Just recap, please." My head was spinning. I needed to hear it, out loud. Someone had to tell me what happened. It all seemed so surreal. I had been in denial. This was what I needed to get to the next stage.

"Your ex went to his mistress's house to break it off. He decided to live a boring life with you, rather than dwell happily with her. They argued. He left and went home to cook dinner. Elizabeth followed him to your house and tried to seduce him. He turned her down. She threatened to expose him. They fought. He stabbed her with a knife from your kitchen and dumped her body nearby." He paused to glare at me, "You following?"

I nodded. It was tough to hear it put so bluntly.

"Anyway, Mr. Templeton came home to clean up the mess. You walked in and, well, you know the rest."

I felt nauseas and sweaty. My head went light. I sat down on his chair.

"Take a breath, Susan. You look faint." The detective didn't bother to stand. I'm not even sure that he looked at me. The room spun. He could have been reading for all I knew.

It took a few minutes to catch my breath. "What should I do now?" I asked him.

"Like I said, I'm not your therapist."

I gave him a hopeless look. There was no one else to turn to.

The detective eyed his coffee and gave it a stir. "Most people move," he finally offered.

"What do you mean? Like move on?"

"No. Most people move away after a crime happens in their home. Why don't you try switching scenery? Stay with a friend or check into a hotel or something."

Finally, some real advice. I could work with that – "move," he had said. Energy built in my body. That was something that I could do. It was a tangible goal.

"Okay. I will. I will go home and pack some things and get out of there."

"Okay, bye." He said into his mug, before taking a huge swig, as if to remind me that he didn't give a shit.

*****

I DROVE HOME TRYING NOT TO LET ANY MORE TEARS FALL, but I couldn't stop them. They kept coming, blocking my view of the road. I drove slowly and eventually pulled over to let them fall at their will. There was no sense fighting what so obviously needed to be felt.

I got out of the car and found a telephone pole. My ribs ached from the heavy breath it took to cry. My hands hurt, but I was angry. Tears dried and turned to salt on my face as I kicked the pole. It was a relief to let out the steam that was building within me. The pole could take it. My foot couldn't. My toes throbbed. I stopped the kicking and paced next to my car in a haze.

I don't know how long the tantrum lasted. But, at some point I began to accept what had happened. I got it; my life with Craig had been a lie. Now, I was faced with reality. I had loved a killer. Now, the worst was in the past. I survived. That era was now history.

All I could do now, was move – move on, move away, move forward. Detective Frank, the jerk, was right. I had to make a new life.

My face dried and my mood sobered. Like a robot, I got in the car and back on the road, went home and began packing. Puddles, of course, helped out by peeing on what was left in Craig's closet. She got a treat for that.

As swiftly as I could, I stuffed my car with a bunch of work stuff, clothes and toiletries. Puddles laid down on the passenger seat as if she understood what was happening. "That makes one of us," I told the cat as we pulled out of the driveway.

We drove off and ended up at the Hard Rock Hotel where we got a room. It was a wild place, but it was the closest hotel to the University, so it would have to do. I hid puddles under a bunch of stuff and once everything was in our room, we collapsed on the bed and slept until the next morning.

When I woke up I briefly forgot where I was. Then, the memories came back. This was our first morning alone, Puddles and I. John wasn't there to lean on and reassure me that it would be okay.

I turned on the television for comfort. The morning news anchors told me about the forecast. It was going to be hot, they said. Big surprise!

I gave myself a pep talk, fed Puddles and left the cold, empty hotel room. At a fast pace, my feet whisked me past the chimes of the slot machines and bright lights. As I busted through the front door of the hotel, I found myself face to face with an Italian man in a dark suit.

"Oh, I'm sorry," I looked up at him, breaking out of autopilot mode.

"Where are you off to so fast? The party's inside," he smiled.

"At five am?" I asked.

"Yeah. The party doesn't stop here."

"I've got swim practice."

"Okay, cheree. But, you stop by room 511, later, okay?"

"Okay," I smiled a real smile and watched his back as he strutted into the Hard Rock. He was unreal, this Italian guy. He was living the crazy fun life. That was the life I should have, I thought. *Heck I'm already living in a hotel! Why not have some fun?*

I decided to visit the Hard Rock bar later that night and zipped off to swim practice.

The Hard Rock Hotel was so much closer to school than my house had been. I arrived extra early. I turned off my car and made myself exit the vehicle. *You can do this. Just keep going through the motions. Eventually, it will get better*, I told myself.

I sighed and leaned on the car, closing my eyes.

"You okay?" I heard John's voice before I opened my eyes to look at him. He looked tired, but probably not nearly as ragged as I did.

"I don't know," I responded.

"You weren't home last night," he said softly, stepping in front of me.

"I know. I moved." I continued to lean on the car.

"Really? Where did you move?" He took a step closer, facing me with each foot straddling each of mine. The heat of his body put me at ease while enticing my hormones at the same time.

"The Hard Rock," I said smiling. I'm sure it sounded ridiculous.

His eyebrows rose. "What room?" He touched my jaw with the slightest tip of his finger.

"Wouldn't you like to know." I sighed and closed my eyes again, "You went to my house last night?"

"Yes. I didn't want you to be alone."

"But I shot you down yesterday."

"Yes, and...?"

I shrugged in response and he read my mind.

"My ego is more shatter-proof than you think," he told me. Then, he brushed my cheek with the back of his fingers, "You were right. We are friends. I care about you, Susan."

I opened my eyes, aroused by his final statement, "You do?"

"Yes," He swept his fingers along my lips. They parted and I kissed his fingers. He let them linger under my pucker.

I hadn't planned to do that. It just happened. I leaned forward, causing him to pull his hand back.

My face was close to his. "I think I'm supposed to get through this alone, John. I am a strong and independent woman. I don't need a man to help me."

"No one should have to go through this alone," he told me and looked deep into my eyes. John placed his hands on my shoulders and studied my face.

"But, I don't need a man."

"Of course you don't," he assured me, "But, isn't it more fun with one?" He slid one hand from shoulder down the front of my body, barely brushing the side of my breast. I shivered.

"This is difficult," I said looking at him. My eyes gave me away. I was in need of human contact.

"Why?" he slipped his hands around my waist.

"Because," I began, but I couldn't say it. He was intoxicating. I was high in his presence. He made me feel good and all the bad stuff disappeared.

"Because…" he pressed me.

"The timing is wrong," I told him, hoping that would be enough for him to back off and let me go back to being depressed. That wasn't what I wanted, but it was what I thought I deserved. I felt that I should be condemned to a one-year minimum sentence of misery.

John wasn't taking the bait. "So what? Our timing sucks. But, the heart wants what the heart wants." He pulled me into him and pressed his pelvis to mine.

"That's not your heart," I commented.

"No, it's much bigger," he replied with a grin.

I laughed before trying to compose myself. "So much is all fucked up between us," I told him.

I didn't push him, or his large organ, away. I took pleasure in feeling the energy from his body flowing through mine. He was warm and delicious up close. John's smell made me salivate. I feared I might drool.

"Oh, it's not that bad," He eyes taunted mine. He gave my ear a kiss. My ear burned and my body sizzled.

That did it. Why should I push away someone that makes me feel so good?

I gave him a look of surrender.

John pulled my face to his and kissed me gently. My arms wrapped around his waist and I felt the muscles in his back with my fingers. I drew his body closer to mine. My pulse raced! It was as if nothing had changed. I was still me; boy-crazy, super horny - me.

Our lips parted and I tasted the inside of his mouth. He was even more sexy and delicious than before. John was my savory drug.

We kissed again and I pulled back to see his beautiful, large, kind eyes. My lips turned up.

"I'll see you after practice," I said.

ABOUT THE AUTHOR

Born in the UK, Everly Chappelle is a well-travelled American gal. She now lives in Naples, CA, where she enjoys the warmth of the sunshine, the sound of the ocean waves and the flip-flop world of coastal living. Everly has one son and one husband... and a winning smile. Her world is full of love, whimsy and playtime with her family.

www.ingramcontent.com/pod-product-compliance
Lightning Source LLC
Chambersburg PA
CBHW060138130626
46556CB00006B/2402